MANHUNTERS

TCU Press Books by Elmer Kelton

Dark Thicket
The Day the Cowboys Quit
Elmer Kelton Country: The Short Nonfiction of a Texas Novelist
The Far Canyon
The Good Old Boys
Honor at Daybreak
The Man Who Rode Midnight
Manhunters
Slaughter
The Smiling Country
Stand Proud
The Time It Never Rained
Wagontongue
The Wolf and the Buffalo

Manhunters

A Novel by Elmer Kelton

with an Afterword by Bill Crider

Texas Christian University Press
Fort Worth

Manhunters
by Elmer Kelton

The Texas Tradition Series: Number Twenty-Two
James Ward Lee, Series Editor

First published by Ballantine Books, 1974.

Published by arrangement with Bantam Books,
a division of Bantam Doubleday Dell Publishing Group, Inc.

Library of Congress Cataloging-in-Publication Data

Kelton, Elmer.
The manhunters / Elmer Kelton: with an introduction by the
author and an afterword by Bill Crider.
p. cm. – (Texas tradition series; no. 22)
ISBN 978-0-87565-134-7 (pbk.; alk. paper)
1. Fugitives from justice—Texas—Fiction. 2. Mexican American
men—Texas—Fiction.
I. Kelton, Elmer. Man on the Wagontongue. II. Title. III. Series.
PS3563.A2932M34 1994
813′.54—dc20   94-6499
CIP

TCU Press
P. O. Box 298300
Fort Worth, Texas 76129
817.257.7822
http://www.prs.tcu.edu

To order books: 800.826.8911

Cover Art and Text Designed by Barbara Whitehead

AUTHOR'S NOTE

Though Texas won its independence from Mexico at the battle of San Jacinto in 1836, the racial antagonism and conflict which led to that war between people of Anglo and Mexican blood continued far into the twentieth century. Traces remain today, though in recent decades the differences have most often moved away from overt violence and into the courtrooms and state legislature. Indeed, the percentage of Texas citizens who are of Hispanic heritage grows year by year. In some southern areas of the state, non-Hispanics are the minority.

Manhunters, first published in 1974, was the last in a long series of original paperback novels I wrote for Ballantine Books. The firm had been founded in the early 1950s by a husband-and-wife team, Ian and Betty Ballantine, to whom I owe more than I could ever repay. By 1974 they had sold the company to a conglomerate. I was shifting most of my fictional efforts toward Doubleday, which was becoming my principal publisher.

This novel, which I had been formulating in my mind for several years, was suggested by the true story of Gregorio Cortez, a young Karnes County horseman who was involved in a shooting in 1901 and ended up on the run, touching off what has been described as the biggest manhunt in Texas history. My version is fictional and makes no claim to following the actual Cortez story except in the broadest terms. Even while Cortez was at large, heroic songs — *corridos* — were made up and sung about him in the *cantinas* of southern Texas. The case was exploited by both Anglo and Mexican alike who felt they had cause to fan up racial hatreds. The *corridos* flourished for years and reflected Hispanic condemnation of Anglo officers, particularly the Texas Rangers, who were viewed as the agents of Anglo supremacy and control. Texas professor Americo Paredes gathered many of these verses in a remarkable though one-sided book, *With His Pistol in His Hand*, published by the University of Texas Press in 1958. The Paredes version was used in the making of an outstanding semi-documentary film, *The Ballad of Gregorio Cortez*, in 1983.

In real life, all the fault, all the bigotry, were not on one side. In a time of unreasoning racial antipathies, there was blame enough to go around.

Elmer Kelton
San Angelo, Texas
1994

MANHUNTERS

The editor of the Domingo *Weekly Observer* leaned against the doorjamb and chewed impatiently on an unlighted cigar as he frowned at the lazy street. It was so quiet out there that a Rhode Island Red could hatch a nest of eggs and never be disturbed. What in the hell was a man supposed to write about when nothing ever happened? Beyond births, natural deaths, weddings, and minutes of the commissioners court, he hadn't had a line of live copy in weeks.

People liked a town to be quiet, but they wanted their paper newsy. The two were a hopeless combination. Lately he had seriously considered selling out and moving up to San Antonio, where a newsman could always find something important to write about . . . a shooting, a stabbing, a barroom brawl . . . something to challenge his abilities.

It had been more than a year since he had had a local story that deserved more than half a galley of type. It had been deadly dull here ever since Sheriff Griffin

Holliday and the Texas Rangers had broken up that horse-stealing ring.

Lately he had done what he could to spice up little "nothing" items such as the fact that the sheriff's comely daughter, the charming Tommie Holliday Sadler, was staying in the comfortable home of her parents in Domingo, awaiting her first blessed event under the care of the good Doctor Jones. The editor had reminded his readers that her husband was the handsome and dashing Texas Ranger Kelly Sadler, who had become smitten by the uncommon beauty of the local maiden last year while on assignment here, working with the sheriff in the horsethief case. He had speculated that Domingo could expect Ranger Sadler back in town any day now to claim not only his wife but also a new heir. "We shall soon see," he had written, "what brand of cigars a gallant Ranger buys for his friends."

It was enough to make an honest newsman gag.

Even the damn Mexicans hadn't had a good old-fashioned cutting scrape over in Old Town since back last winter. When a man couldn't even find a good Mexican killing to put in his paper, things had come to a sorry pass.

He shrugged and stepped out into the dirt street toward the courthouse. Well, he would go look at the county record again. When all else failed, a diligent reporter could usually dig up some kind of financial shenanigans in the courthouse. Maybe he could catch the jailer buying smoking tobacco for himself and charging it up to the prisoners' meal fund again. Goddamn a dead town!

2   Chacho Fernandez thought it was the prettiest day he had seen since the spring grass had turned green and the mesquites had put on their leaves. It had rained yesterday, but now the sun was out and the sky was all clear and blue. The air had a fresh-washed smell, scented a little by the white and yellow blossoms of the wildflowers. By summer they would turn into bothersome weeds, but that was not a thing to trouble a man now. Altogether it was a beautiful morning that made a man glad this land was his home, that

this was the time the good Father had chosen to let Chacho Fernandez be young.

He had no sixth sense to tell him this would be the most terrible day of his life.

On the wagon road ahead of him a dozen ponies were stretched out in a slow trot, their hoofs leaving deep prints in the two wheel-worn ruts but raising no dust because of yesterday's one-inch rain. Chacho hung back a little so the trailing horses would not kick wads of wet sand into his face.

Chacho's brother Felix rode beside him in the right-hand wagon rut, his brown face sober. Pretty June mornings brought him no joy; he had worked too long for the gringos, and had picked up some of their ways. A handful of silver might make him smile, but a sunny sky never would.

"Cheer up, Felix," Chacho said. "Today all these broncs are broken. Today the sorrel mare will be mine."

Felix shook his head. "And what if tomorrow she breaks her leg or cuts herself on the barbed wire? What will you have then? Better you had taken money for the job, and gotten some of it in advance."

"I would only have spent the money to buy the sorrel mare, or another like her. What is money except to buy what you want?"

Felix shook his head. "You will be a poor man all your life."

"Perhaps," Chacho grinned, "but I will always ride a good horse."

In truth, the sorrel mare was not to be for himself. For more than a month now he had ridden these dozen broncs every day and had taken their abuse and their bruises. Once he had been thrown into a fence and knocked half unconscious, but that was all right. All had been done in the hope that the sorrel mare would be a gift pleasing in the eyes of Luisa Aguilar.

Luisa was the daughter of Baudelio Aguilar, who rent-cropped a small farm twenty-five or thirty miles to the northward, across the line in the next county. Last summer when Chacho could not find work punching cattle or

3

breaking horses he had gone over in that direction to stay with his old friends the Bustamante family and to chop cotton for the gringo farmers. He had intended to stay only a few weeks and then return home to see if more respectable work had opened up. But chance had brought his eyes to fall upon the slender form and lovely face of doe-eyed Luisa, a neighbor to the Bustamantes. He had stayed through cotton-picking season and nearly to Christmas, when all the cotton was out and there was no longer any valid excuse for him to remain.

There had been an understanding of sorts between him and Luisa by then. Old Baudelio had seemed in favor of it. Each time he had married off a daughter he had lightened the burden upon himself, and God knew the burden had been heavy. But the old señora had shown little favor. All summer and fall she had been a relentless chaperone, never letting Chacho carry Luisa out of her sight except when some other trusted person was there.

Some of the older daughters had married men who had little more of the world's goods than Chacho. The old lady had given up hard at each wedding but had bowed to inevitability and had hoped her Luisa, the fairest of them all, should do better. Her beauty should at least bring her a match with a storekeeper in town, a man who could build her a house large enough that she and her husband would not have to share even their bedroom with the children who in God's grace would surely come. She was dismayed when Luisa's eyes brightened to the handsome face and the easy, uneducated talk of this rootless *vaquero*, this shirtless cotton-picker Chacho, who had no steady job of his own but lived much of the time at the ranch where his brother worked, eating the patron's food, doing work without pay for his brother's patron in exchange for the courtesy, doing outside work anywhere he could find it.

It was at Easter that Chacho had promised Luisa a good horse. He had made the long ride to visit and go with her to Mass, hoping this gesture might help prove to the old señora that he was not in league with the devil. He found

4

the whole family walking from the farm into town for church: one of their mules had taken down with a bellyache and could not be used to pull the wagon. Chacho had told Luisa she would not have to walk again, that the next time he came he would bring her a fine horse that she could have for her own.

Thus it was that when the gringo horse-trader Barnhill offered him the chance to saddle-break a dozen green broncs, Chacho was pleased to take him up. Chacho had seen a pretty young mare in Barnhill's corral, a sorrel with three stocking feet and a little streak down her nose. He had not even asked Barnhill how much she was worth in cash; he had simply offered to break the' dozen broncs in return for the mare. This was one of the points that had so disturbed Chacho's brother Felix. Chacho should have asked the price first; perhaps it was less than what the breaking of the broncs would pay. But that was not Chacho's way. He was not one to haggle and wheedle and bargain. Money was only an intermediate step. If he could get what he wanted by direct trade and eliminate the artificial handling of money, why not do so? A man was meant for higher things in this world than to count pieces of silver.

Felix grumbled, "There is probably something wrong with the mare. With money all you have to do is count it; either it is all there or it is not. When you agree beforehand about the money, that is one time the gringo cannot cheat you."

"Why should he cheat me?"

"He is a gringo is he not? A gringo will always cheat you."

Chacho snorted. "You sound like old Esteban Bustamante or that Baltazar Fierro, who calls himself a lawyer. They are both always shouting about how one day all us Mexicanos must rise up and drive the gringos back off of our land."

"It would be a far better country if they had never come."

"But they did come, and the land is theirs, most of it. We can never change that."

"We might."

"Anyway, how much of the land did we ever own? None. Even in the old times it belonged to the rich, not to the poor people. What difference if it belongs to the gringos instead of to Mexican *ricos*? At least they do not make peóns of us."

"Don't they? Does breaking a dozen ponies not seem a lot of work to do for one little mare?"

"Not for this mare, and for what this mare will get for me."

"And if you do get a girl foolish enough to give herself to you for a sorrel mare, what then? You will need a place to live. You will have to feed her, and the children that come. You will wish a thousand times you had taken the money instead of the mare."

Chacho did not expect Felix to understand. To Felix a horse was simply a thing to use for getting where one wanted to go; a mule would do as well. Nor did Felix share Chacho's strong feeling for beautiful women. Felix had contented himself with a plumpish wife who lacked much of being beautiful, though she was a good cook. Felix was fonder of the table than of the bed.

Still several miles out of Domingo, Chacho heard a shout on the road behind him and turned in the saddle. "Stagecoach is coming. We had better move the horses out of the road."

He spurred up, yelling pleasant obscenities at the young broncs, moving them off into the tall grass and the low brush that hugged tight against the roadside.

Stagecoach was a grandiose word for the low-slung mud-wagon that carried the mail and usually a passenger or two on this long, winding route through mesquite and cactus country far south of San Antonio. It was a flat-topped rig with open sides, and canvas flaps that could be rolled down in the rare spells of inclement weather . . . this was a country that seldom had more than half as much rain as it needed. Chacho had never ridden in a stagecoach himself and never expected to. In his view it was something only for the rich gringos; not even the working gringos could afford it except in a case of dire emergency, and the Mexicans never could. He turned to see what manner of rich *gueros* were riding the coach today. Probably a landowner or two, and perhaps some politicians. All politicians were rich, he was certain; most of them had smooth hands and long fingers, the better to reach deep into the tax coffers.

He was disappointed to see only one man besides the driver. Well, he thought, perhaps times were getting hard even for the gringo. He lifted his hand in greeting, not really expecting a return gesture. But the lone passenger gave him a sort of salute, and a half-hearted smile that made Chacho take a better look. This was a man not many years older than himself. A stern brown mustache and the square set of his shoulders gave him the look of authority, even before Chacho noticed the round piece of metal pinned to the man's shirt. He knew that badge and felt a chill. That was a Texas Ranger badge.

Mexican people from San Antonio south to the Rio Grande dreaded the Texas *rinches*. Chacho had heard many stories. He could not recall that he had ever been harmed by a Ranger or had ever seen anybody harmed by one. He could not think of anyone he personally knew who ever had been, unless perhaps it was that lying old smuggler Julio Carrasco, who claimed to have been pistol-whipped by the Rangers once in Laredo. But Chacho knew that Julio was bad to cheat at cards. Probably he had been caught and chastised by his opponents; the Ranger story was likely a convenient fiction designed to help cover the truth of the matter.

Nevertheless it was an article of faith among the people of the lower country that the Rangers were an oppressive force whose chief dedication it was to keep them in a position of servitude, somewhere a few steps above the black but several steps beneath the gringo. Chacho had long since decided there must be some truth in it, otherwise so many of the people would not declare it to be so.

He noted after the mud-wagon passed him that the Ranger took a long, careful look at the broncs as he came even with them by ones and twos. Probably this lawman had an eye for horses, Chacho thought at first. Then a second thought came to him, a disturbing one. Perhaps the Ranger was studying the brands, convinced the horses were stolen.

Many horses were regularly stolen from the ranches in this section of the country. It was no secret that some of the Mexican cowboys were among the most skillful of thieves. They saw it as no crime, many of them. They regarded it as a just revenge against the gringos who had taken over this formerly Mexican land. Not even a priest could show most of them the wrong in it. It was, in a way, a holy mission.

Chacho himself had engaged in the traffic awhile, but he had quit long before the officers' big drive last year against the thieves and the "line." He had let that revolutionary old fire-eater Esteban Bustamante convince him it was his duty as a man to do whatever he could to chastise the American. It was not stealing when one took from these *extranjeros*, it was a form of guerrilla warfare, a patriotic duty on the part of one who believed in *la raza*, the race, the people. Chacho had made many trips down the line, down those hidden trails from the Bustamante place to Julio Carrasco's on the Rio Grande. He had finally become disillusioned when he saw that all the glory went to those like himself who assumed the risks, but the profits went to people like the lawyer Fierro, who arranged the sales and took few chances. The officers had killed several good men last year, but Fierro went right on, undiscovered.

Chacho had decided that patriotism too often hinged upon money, and that breaking broncs and chopping cotton carried far less risk.

The coach rolled on without stopping. The driver was an Americano whose face Chacho knew, although not his name. Probably the driver knew *his* face, too, and was telling the Ranger that he saw these Mexicans often around Domingo and doubted that they were up to any evil.

Chacho loped ahead of the horses and eased them back into the road, where they were less likely to stray off on a tangent. He reined to a stop and waited for Felix to come up even with him.

Felix said darkly, "Did you see the *rinche*?"

"I saw."

"He gave us a good looking-over. I think he would have liked to shoot both of us."

"That is a foolish notion. He never even tried to stop."

"Perhaps he did not want the driver to witness."

Chacho saw no gain in arguing. The old notions were too deeply burned into his brother's mind.

Felix said, "You know how they train the Rangers, don't you?"

Chacho shook his head. "How?"

"Before they will give them the star they take them to the state capital in San Antonio. . . ."

"The state capital is in Austin."

"No matter. They take them to the state capital and tell them all the things they are supposed to learn. Then before they will give them the star each man has to go out upon the streets and shoot three Mexicans. When he has killed his three, then he gets his star."

That Chacho could not let go unchallenged. "I have never heard anything so foolish."

"Nevertheless, it is true. I have heard it from people who know."

Chacho shrugged. There was no way to talk to people who would not listen.

The town of Domingo was old, but not in its present form. There had been a little Mexican settlement here for a hundred years or more, way back into the time when Texas and even Mexico herself was still a part of Spain. That is, it belonged to Spain, and most of the people in it belonged to one rich Spaniard or another. They were not slaves in the full sense of the word, as if they had been black. If they could ever pay all their debts to the patron they were free men. But of course the system was so neatly arranged that a

9

peón was born with a heavy debt on his shoulders, and as the shoulders grew wider, the debt grew also. For most, the only release was in the grave, or, for some, simply running away to live the life of an outlaw. So eventually Mexico had rebelled and won her freedom by war, the same way the *yanquis* had won their freedom from the *ingleses*. But one tyranny took the place of another, and a time came when the Texan immigrants rose up in fury and beat hell out of Santa Anna. Then Texas was no longer a part of Mexico.

Chacho had heard these stories from the old men ever since he could remember. He had always enjoyed hearing the part about the fighting, but the political aspects had never moved him much one way or the other. It seemed to him that the poor people had been under someone's domination as far back as the old men's stories reached. That, he figured, was the way life was for poor people all over the world.

He pondered about the best way to get the horses through Domingo and raise the least fuss. The local merchants would not appreciate having the ponies trail down the main street, scattering their customers and causing general inconvenience. They would probably complain to the authorities, who would levy a fine heavy enough to take the sorrel mare away from him. If he drove the horses along one of the lesser streets he would probably stir up some of the local housewives, but their complaints would be carried only to their husbands. If he had to upset somebody, it was better he upset the wives. None of them, after all, were his.

He loped up ahead of the broncs to take the lead to the trader Barnhill's corrals at the far edge of town. Felix would stay behind and push the ponies. Chacho veered off the main road and onto a gringo residential street.

He had always considered Domingo a pretty town. Its streets — except the very oldest — had been laid out wide enough that a teamster could turn several spans of oxen around without having to stop and back up. This was an Anglo touch; the old streets which dated to the Spanish and Mexican time were narrow and pinched, an economy of space in a land that had all the room in the world. Perhaps, Chacho thought, the Mexican teamsters always knew where they were going — never changed their minds and had to turn around.

The frame houses of the Anglos stood in strong contrast to the squat adobes and rock homes and the poor brush-walled *jacales* of the Mexican section in Old Town. Chacho looked up in wonder at the wires stretched along the edge of the street on poles which reminded him of the cross where the Christ had been crucified. It was said these wires could carry the human voice to far-off places, so that a man in San Antonio could talk to a man in Domingo as if they stood face to face. Chacho had seen the strange box on the wall at one of the stores, a box with a bell and ugly-looking wires hanging down and around something that stuck out from the front. He had seen men stand close and shout into this box as if it had ears but was a touch deaf, but he had never heard the box answer back. It was said voices came out of the little black tube the gringos held to their ears, but Chacho could not vouch for this with any personal authority. He had never been invited to listen.

It might be that the boxes spoke only English anyway; Chacho knew no Mexican who claimed ever to have talked to one except Fierro. If that was the case, Chacho was out of luck; he knew only a limited amount of English, certainly not enough to carry on a conversation with a box which had no eyes, no expression which might help bring him the meaning of the words which went over his head.

Some of the old men said there was nothing to the boxes; they were only a trick to help the Mexican people think the Americans were so much smarter. And indeed it was a thing to make a man wonder. It was said the wires were solid. Had they been hollow Chacho might find the concept easier to believe, for he knew that a man could shout into one end of a long pipe and be heard plainly at the other end. But voices on a solid wire . . . that took much faith.

Yet he reasoned that the device must actually work

because otherwise no gringo would willingly spend money stringing wires and putting these boxes on their walls. Certainly not any he had ever met.

At the second corner he saw two men standing on a front porch. He realized this was the home of the county sheriff, Griffin Holliday. He had not thought of the sheriff's house when he had chosen this street to drive the horses. It was fortunate that yesterday's rain held down the dust, or the *cherife* might put him under arrest for creating a nuisance. At the sound of the horses the sheriff turned, his eyes searching in interest.

Chacho saw no menace in the officer's attitude. Holliday, a man far into his fifties, was starting to sag a little in the shoulders and bulge a little at his belt, as befitted a man who had done his work well and now harvested the fruits of a life's labor. Holliday had a reputation among the Mexican people that he was firm but not unfair. He demanded respect for the law but was not normally arbitrary in his handling of it unless he was crossed. In such an event he had a temper that rose quickly to the flash point, and everybody had better step out of his way.

A man who minded his own business had little to fear from such a *cherife*, Chacho was sure.

He recognized the other man on the porch. He was the passenger who had been on the stage, the Ranger. It was a natural thing for a *rinche* to stop by and visit a *cherife*. Probably they were comparing notes on some wanted criminal.

Chacho took off his hat and gave the two lawmen a pleasant nod as he rode by. The sheriff nodded in return.

It is good, he thought, *that I have no trouble with those two.*

TWO

Griffin Holliday stood with his hands shoved deep into his pockets and stared across the front yard at the young horses trotting by in the street. "Good-lookin' set of broncs, most of them."

Kelly Sadler nodded. "I passed them on the road. Gotten so I can't come into this section of the country any more without takin' a hard look at the brand on every horse I see. Reflex, I guess."

"They belong to that horse-trader Barnhill, out at the edge of town. Seen them in his corrals awhile back before he farmed them out to a Mexican *jinete* to be saddle-broke for him."

"Those hombres didn't look like horsethieves to me."

A half-smile tugged at the corners of Griffin Holliday's mostly gray mustache. "What does a horsethief look like, Kelly? If you can tell me, you'll save me a lot of false starts." The heavy-set sheriff cast a moment's gaze toward Chacho Fernandez, up ahead of the broncs, and then back to Felix Fernandez, coming along slowly in the rear. "Far as I know, them two boys have never been a problem to anybody. They hold down a camp on old man Frisco's ranch. Damned if I remember their names . . . Hernandez or Hernando or somethin' like that . . . never did have much knack for them Mexican names."

The young Ranger turned his back on the horses, his interest in them gone. "You real sure Tommie's all right? She doesn't look too good."

"Doc says she's fine. We wouldn't've sent for you, even, if it hadn't looked like her time had come. False labor. Time we found out, you were already on the way."

Kelly looked worriedly through the front door. His wife lay asleep in the back bedroom; they had decided not to awaken her when he arrived, so he had sneaked a quiet look and retreated. "I shouldn't've let her talk me into sendin' her here, Griff. It's been a lot of trouble for you-all."

"Her mother wouldn't've had it any other way. She was our daughter long before she was your wife. Havin' her home has been like a tonic."

Kelly stared at his father-in-law's considerable bulk and smiled again. "Don't look to me like you need much tonic."

The sheriff rubbed his ample belly. "Things've been so quiet lately, there ain't been enough exercise to keep me from runnin' to fat."

Kelly Sadler studied the aging sheriff with affection for a kinsman and respect for a good peace officer. Griffin Holliday understood people, and this had been one of his strengths. He usually knew when to be patient and when to be firm, when to believe and when to be skeptical. In many a long ride and many a patience-grinding interrogation, Kelly had seldom found Griff wrong. Where reason did not suffice, instinct carried him the extra way. If he had a shortcoming, it was his short-fused temper that flared when he met resistance. Holliday held a deeply ingrained conviction that the law was right even when it was wrong, that it was first and last and always to be *obeyed*. If it was to be questioned, that questioning was to be done in court, *not* against the enforcing or arresting officer. He believed that if the enforcing officer did not do his duty, then the law at all other levels was useless and without respect.

Looking into the weather-browned, hard-lined face of Griffin Holliday, Kelly could see features Holliday had bequeathed to his daughter — the same eyes, the same determined set of the chin. Because Kelly loved his wife, he had to love this formidable old man who was her father.

"You ever thought about retirin', Griff?"

"And do what?"

"Raise cattle . . . horses. You're a good hand with stock."

"Why should I want to retire from this business?"

"It can be dangerous, once in a while."

"I've never backed away from duty in my life."

"But you've put in your time. You've earned a right to spend the rest of your life workin' for Griff Holliday and not for the public."

"The public's been good to me."

"Not *all* the public. You're carryin' your share of scars. You're not gettin' any younger. One of these days you'll come upon somebody who's young and fast, and he'll hurt you."

"You thinkin' I'm too old?"

"'Not yet, but soon. Quit while you're ahead, Griff."

Holliday grunted. "I'll think about it . . . when I get *old*." His attention shifted to a wagon coming up the street. "You think retirement is easy for a man who's always been active? Take a look at old Joe Florey yonder."

Kelly turned quickly, his eyes widening a little. "Old Tracker Joe?" He squinted, trying better to see the man sitting hunch-shouldered on the wagon seat, the leather lines in his hands. A young Mexican boy sat beside him. Behind them, in the wagon bed, was a load of lumber.

Kelly said, "I can't tell much about him at the distance. Is he doin' all right?"

"He eats regular . . . don't lack for money, particularly. But I wouldn't say he's doin' all right. He's bitter, Kelly."

Kelly frowned. "Against me, I guess."

"Against you . . . and others."

Kelly had known Joe Florey hadn't taken kindly to a forced retirement from the Rangers, but he had hoped he would get over the resentment and realize it had been for his own good. "What's he doin' with the lumber, buildin' a house?"

"No, he's carpenterin' when he can find anything to do. Nights, he's a watchman. Bunch of the merchants pay him to keep an eye on their places. But when a man has spent thirty-forty years in the Rangers, and been respected from one end of the state to the other, it's a bad step-down to go around rattlin' doors."

The wagon passed. Joe Florey gave Griff Holliday a nod, but his gaze touched Kelly Sadler and quickly cut away. He had nothing for Kelly, not even a *go-to-hell.*

Holliday said, "You got to see it from his standpoint. He feels like they used him up and threw him out like an old pair of boots."

"I'm not the one that said he had to quit."

"But they asked your opinion."

"I couldn't lie. I had to tell them he like to've gotten himself and a couple more of us killed because he was too slow. It wasn't fair to himself or to the men who had to work with him. It's not his fault the years caught up with him."

"He's still one of the best trackers the good Lord ever put on this earth. He could trail an eagle by the mark its shadow leaves."

"But he was already a grown man trailin' Comanches for one of the frontier companies way back in the first year or two of the Confederacy. You were just a big kid then, and I wasn't even born."

"But they owe him for that. They owe him more than to turn him out to grass with a little bitty pension and tell him he isn't no use any more. Worst thing of all is, he's got to doubtin' himself, Kelly. Times, I think he wishes they'd killed him in the line of duty. Maybe Texas would've put up a monument to him instead of throwin' him away."

"They offered him a job in the state office."

"Sittin' behind some desk, like an exhibit in a sideshow? Bad as it is, he's probably better off rattlin' doors."

Kelly's eyes narrowed. "All the more reason, Griff, that you ought to do somethin' else yourself."

Chacho Fernandez loped up ahead of the broncs and swung down easily at the front gate of Barnhill's corrals. He opened the slide latch and gave the gate a hard push inward. He remounted and moved out a little way to help haze the horses into the pen. A bay that had held the lead all the way to town went through the gate without a sign of reluctance, and the others followed him. Felix reined up just outside as Chacho dismounted again and went in to shut the gate.

Though it was only a short walk around to the barn, Chacho got back on his horse. Cowboys — Anglo or Mexican — seldom walked twenty steps if they could ride instead.

He looked around for the sorrel mare that was to be his. She stood in a far pen, her head poked over a fence and ears pointed in interest toward the newly arrived broncs. A brown mare shared the pen with her. *Ay*, but she was a pretty thing, that sorrel, well worth the work he had invested. He would pick up a bottle before he left town; he had much to celebrate.

Barnhill stepped lazily out of the barn, casting a dubious eye at Chacho and Felix, then moved to the corral. He stooped and peered between the sun-grayed one-by-eight planks. "Been lookin' for you the last several days," he said with a touch of complaint. "'Bout decided you'd run off with my horses."

Chacho strained a little to get the full meaning of the words and hoped they weren't meant to carry the accusation he read into them. English was a difficult language at best, and even more difficult to understand when it was delivered in Barnhill's slurring run-together of words. Chacho replied in Spanish, knowing Barnhill could under-

17

stand him. "I did not want to bring them in until I could guarantee them. This brown I am riding is the gentlest. See how well he reins?"

Chacho demonstrated the pony's response to a tug of the hackamore reins and pulled up with pride. "How is that? Is that not good?"

"One horse don't prove the lot," Barnhill said. "I believe I'll want to see you ride another one or two before I say whether you've done the job or not."

Felix hung back, not understanding the trader's words and gathering only their general meaning by Chacho's answers and reactions. Felix was not fond of trafficking with gringos more than he had to anyway. Of course he worked for wages for old man Frisco, who was a pretty good sort as gringos went. He demanded that you do your allotted work but always paid what he had agreed to and never bawled you out within the hearing of your friends or family.

Barnhill was nowhere near so pleasant. He had a way of being always above the man he talked to. He was known to curse a man in the midst of a crowd. That robbed a man of his dignity, often the only thing he had in the first place.

Chacho opened a gate near the barn and led the brown into the corral where the broncs had been placed. He dropped his big-horned Mexico saddle gently to the earth, then slipped the hackamore off and turned the horse loose to trot across the pen and rejoin its compadres. He took the long, thin maguey rope from his saddle and stepped across the sandy lot toward the broncs. He shook out a long loop, swung it in front of him and then back in an underhanded motion that sent it swirling around the neck of the bay that instinctively always took the lead. The bay snorted, but not enough to show any serious rebellion against authority. Chacho picked up the hackamore and started slowly up the rope.

Barnhill called out. "No you don't. You *would* catch out the gentlest in the bunch. Turn that one loose and catch the dun."

Chacho couldn't remember what the word *dun* meant until Barnhill curtly informed him what a stupid damn Mexican he was and pointed out the one he wanted. Swallowing a growing anger, Chacho roped the dun. Humping, it acted at first as if it might pitch. But Chacho put it to trotting back and forth across the pen, and shortly the hump disappeared. The horse did not rein so easily as the brown, but it did well enough for one barely halter-broken. He stepped down quickly and carefully because now that the hump was gone the girth was loose and the saddle could turn.

Chacho no longer made any effort at friendliness. All he wanted was to get his sorrel mare and get the hell away. "This one is the poorest of them all, and he is not bad, as you can see."

Barnhill shook his head. "As good as a man can expect, considerin' the people he has to depend on." He turned and walked back to the barn, not looking behind him.

Grinding his teeth and trying to chew away his anger, Chacho unsaddled the horse and turned it loose. He had done a first-class job on these broncs, and he knew it. Why did it always seem to hurt one of these coyote-eyed gringos so much to admit that a man had done his work well? He wondered if he would ever understand these people.

Bueno, there was no use wasting time around here. There was nothing in this place he wanted except the sorrel mare. He picked up his rope, walked into the pen where she was and stood a moment admiring her before he swung the loop and dropped it gently around her neck. He gave only a glance to the brown mare in the pen. She was common, a little cathammed, with none of the eagle look in the eye which had first attracted him to the sorrel. The brown might do to breed to a jack and produce a mule to pull a plow, but that was all she was good for.

The sorrel mare came easily to Chacho after she felt the pull of the rope. He spoke quietly and rubbed her neck and her foreshoulder and looked her over to see if she had any blemishes he might have missed before. She was as near perfect as a man could want.

He knew she was bridle-broken, but because he had ridden a bronc to town he had no bridle or bits with him; he had only the hackamore which fitted over the head and around the nose. One did not put bits into a pony's mouth until it first had learned to respond to the hackamore. He kept talking to her. He had always believed a man's voice was important in the training of an animal, be it horse or dog. A rough voice brought resistance. A gentle voice earned gentleness.

"Luisa is going to love you. I had better give you to her quickly or I may decide to keep you myself "

He led her into the pen where he had left his saddle. He was tightening the girth when he heard Barnhill demand angrily, "Hey, hombre, what do you think you're doin'?"

Chacho turned, blinking in surprise, alarm coming up like red beans rising in boiling water. "I am saddling my mare."

"Your mare hell! What gave you the idea this is your mare?"

The beans were at full boil, suddenly. Chacho stepped away from the mare, his tough brown hands going instinctively into fists. "This is my mare. I have earned her. You promised her to me for breaking your broncs."

"I promised you *a* mare," Barnhill said sharply. "I didn't tell you which one. You're takin' that brown mare in yonder."

Chacho felt the blood hot in his face. He trembled in the flash of anger, the first full sense of betrayal. "It was made plain from the beginning. We discussed it well. I said I would do the work for this sorrel mare, and you agreed. That brown mare was not even here."

Barnhill shouted, "Don't you sass me, you damn chili picker! You'll take the mare I tell you to take, and no other!"

Barnhill reached for Chacho's saddle, but Chacho reached for Barnhill. He caught a fistful of the man's blue shirt and pushed him back. "This is my mare! You will not rob me, gringo. The law will stand behind me."

Barnhill gripped Chacho's hand and pulled it loose from his shirt, his gray eyes crackling. That Chacho had touched him seemed to enrage him more than Chacho's taking the mare. "The law? You think the law will take your word against mine? You pull that saddle off or I'll have you throwed in jail as a horsethief. Understand me, chili? I said *horsethief*."

Chacho's understanding of English had suddenly improved. "There is a thief here, and it is not me. Step out of my way or I will run over you."

Felix sat on his horse outside the fence, his mouth and eyes wide open. He made a move as if to come in and help, but Chacho waved him back. "You stay outside, Felix. This is for *me* to do."

Barnhill made a grab at the hackamore rein.

Chacho knew full well what the penalty could be for a Mexican who took it upon himself to strike a gringo. He knew that any extenuating circumstances had to be massive indeed for public opinion to justify him. But this moment he was interested in justifying nothing to anyone but himself. He swung his fist with all the strength he had.

The impact was so hard and the sound so sharp that for a moment Chacho thought he had broken the trader's neck. He would not have cared except for the difficulties such an eventuality was sure to bring. Barnhill lay stunned, blood running from his cut lip. He raised his head and shook it. Chacho had not broken his neck after all. A pity.

Felix's eyes were wide in fright. "You will be in much trouble over this. I told you this gringo would cheat you out of what is yours."

"He has not cheated me. I am taking what is mine."

He finished tightening the girth and swung up into the saddle. He cast one more contemptuous glance at the horsetrader, who had raised up into a sitting position. "You had better give me no trouble, Barnhill, or I will tell them who is the thief."

He rode quickly out of the corral and started to spur away but remembered the open gate. It was in his *vaquero* training not to leave a gate open, not even an enemy's gate. He stepped down and closed it so the broncs would not escape past Barnhill. Firmly he shut the latch and remounted the sorrel mare. He gave not another glance to Barnhill but instead reined the mare around the corral and put her into a gentle, swinging lope toward the town.

Gone now was any thought of a drink. He was much too angry to add more fire to his blood.

He followed the tracks the broncs had made as he and Felix had brought them through the streets. Ahead was the sheriff's house. He saw the two men still sitting on the porch. He gave the Ranger only a quick glance, for this was a man he did not know. But he knew the heavy-set sheriff and thought perhaps if any gringo would understand, this man would.

Chacho reined up at the fence and shouted at the graying man on the porch. "Señor *cherife!* I have stolen nothing. I have taken only what is mine."

He pulled the mare around and spurred into a lope down the street, leaving the startled sheriff to stare after him in wonderment.

THREE

Griffin Holliday walked to the edge of his porch and watched the two Mexicans disappear around the corner at the end of the street. "Kelly, did you hear what he said?"

"He said he hadn't stolen anything . . . just took what belonged to him."

"That's what I thought he said, but I don't follow that lingo any too good." He turned back to the Ranger, his heavy mustache drooping. "Reckon what the hell he meant by that?"

Kelly Sadler raised up from his chair and walked slowly to the door, listening for some stirring that might mean his wife was awake. The two Mexicans meant nothing to him. He had no particular jurisdiction in local affairs unless they were beyond the ability of the local authorities to cope. He was only bothered by the idea that the man's shouting might have brought Tommie out of a badly needed sleep.

The sheriff rubbed his jaw. "Maybe I ought to catch up

to them and see what the matter is. If there's been trouble I ought to know about it."

"Time you could catch and saddle a horse they'll have two miles start on you. I didn't hear any shootin'."

Holliday settled his portly form back into his chair, stretching his legs out in front of him. "You ever come to a point that you understand them people, Kelly?"

"I'm not sure I understand anybody."

"Mexicans, they don't look at things like other people. They'll fight over some little thing that nobody else would pay attention to. Then somethin'll come up that'd send me and you runnin' for a gun, and they'll just laugh about it. I'm damned if I understand their ways."

"I suppose we all look odd to somebody." Sadler kept gazing at the screen door until he couldn't stand it. "I'm goin' in and take a look at her, Griff. If she's asleep I'll be back in a minute."

"Take your time. I ain't goin' no place."

Kelly Sadler tiptoed through the front parlor and the kitchen to a back bedroom. He stopped in the doorway and stared at the still form lying covered by a thin blanket, her long brown hair spread in disarray on the white pillow, framing a face that to him was the prettiest he had ever seen. Tommie continued to sleep. He was relieved, in a way, yet he almost wished she had awakened. He fought down an impulse to kiss her. That would wake her up. He made his way back to the porch. There he sat again, half listening for a sound from the house, half listening to Griffin Holliday telling an old story about an outlaw who had been hell to catch, fifteen or twenty years ago.

24 His eye was caught, finally, by a buggy coming down the street at a good clip, its thin iron tires flinging up clusters of sand still cohesive from yesterday's rain. Griffin Holliday groaned a little. "I had a feelin' I ought to've gone after them Mexicans. Now it'll be a right smart more of a ride."

Kelly saw no connection between the two horsemen and this buggy, but he accepted the fact that Griff did. He recognized one of Holliday's deputies in the driver's seat. He did not know the other man.

Griffin said, "That's Barnhill. He's holdin' himself like somethin' has happened to him. Son of a bitch needs a good killin'."

Deputy Sheriff Odom Willcox shouted as he pulled the team to a halt, "We got trouble, Griff."

Holliday grumbled that he already knew it and hobbled heavily down the two short steps from the porch to the ground. Kelly Sadler followed. The deputy's eyes shifted momentarily to him in surprise. "Howdy, Sadler. Didn't know you was in town. We may need you."

Holliday said gruffly, "His wife needs him; we don't." He looked impatiently at the trader, hunched on the buggy seat. "What is it, Barnhill? What mess have you got yourself into this time?"

Deputy Willcox didn't give Barnhill much chance to speak. "Horsethieves, Griff. They beat poor old Jim almost to a pulp and left him for dead. Probably thought he was dead or they'd of finished him."

Kelly stared critically at Barnhill's face. He could see some swelling and a deep cut on his lower lip, but he saw no sign that the man was all that much in danger of death.

The sheriff said curtly, "Dammit, Odom, they didn't cut his tongue out, did they? Let him speak for himself."

The split lip was a handicap to Barnhill in forming his words. "The two Fernandez brothers, Griff, they tried to kill me. They beat me and then taken a sorrel mare out of my corral."

Holliday glanced at Kelly Sadler. Kelly nodded. He remembered that the one who had shouted at Griff had been riding a sorrel mare.

The deputy said excitedly, "I sent Farris Elam to gather up some men. We'll have them horsethieves in an hour or we'll know the reason why!"

Holliday's face began to color. He raised both hands. "Now you just calm down a little, Odom. I'll decide if I want any extra help or not. A lot of extra men and advice is generally the last thing I need." His sharp gaze cut back to Barnhill. "Them two Mexican boys come by here while ago. One of them made a point to tell me he hadn't stolen anything; he just taken what belonged to him. Maybe you can explain what he was talkin' about, Barnhill." He wasn't asking him; he was demanding.

"He's just another damn Mexican, sheriff, and you know these Mexicans."

"No, I don't. Suppose you tell me about them."

"They never tell the truth when a lie will do. He liked that mare and he taken her; that's all there was to it."

Deputy Willcox nodded, a strong air of excitement carrying him along. "They'll do it to you every time."

Holliday's eyes seemed to be cutting a hole through Barnhill. "I get a feelin' when a man's lyin' to me. Right now I ain't sure which lie to believe — yours or that Mexican's. You real certain he didn't have a right to that mare?"

Barnhill reacted with resentment. "I'm tellin' you, ain't I?"

"I'll put it to you plain, Barnhill. I never thought much of you. I've seen the outcome of too many of your horse-trades. I keep askin' myself why that Mexican would've rode by here to tell me what he did. If he'd stolen that mare, the last person he would want to see would be a sheriff."

Barnhill's eyes were murderous. "You takin' that Mexican's word against mine?"

"I ain't taken' either of you at your word."

The deputy stared incredulously at the sheriff. "Griff, look at old Jim! They like to've killed him. You take that as the work of an honest man?"

26

"I've seen some honest men that would love to've done it."

Barnhill's fists were knotted. He looked to Kelly Sadler for support, but Kelly stood with his arms folded as a way of indicating that he had no stake in this one way or the other. "Sheriff," the trader said after a moment of hostile silence, "that mare is mine. I want her back, and I want to see that Mexican in jail."

Odom Willcox said with too much eagerness, "I'll take care of this for you, Griff. I'll go bring him in."

The sheriff gave him a sharp glance. "I'll bet you would, Odom. Dead or alive. Probably dead."

"I wouldn't kill him unless I had to."

"Yes, I know. But I'd prefer you stay here and look after things. I'll go."

Willcox protested. "You can't go out there all by yourself. Them Mexicans get a chance, they'll kill you."

Kelly spoke for the first time. "I'll go with you, Griff."

Griffin Holliday considered his son-in-law a minute, then turned him down. "Your place is here with Tommie. This is my county and my responsibility." He glanced back to Odom Willcox. "Go find Albert Stout for me. Tell him to bring my buggy and meet me here soon as he can. I'll take Albert along to interpret for me."

Willcox patted the butt of the pistol high on his hip. "This is all the interpretation you need for them people."

Holliday shouted in anger, "You goin' or not?"

"I'm goin'."

"Fine. And take Barnhill with you. Be damned if I want to look at him." He shoved his big stubby finger in Bamhill's face. "If I find out you're the one that's lyin', I will be lookin' at you through the bars of a cell."

Barnhill didn't need help to climb back into the buggy; he seemed glad to get away.

Kelly offered again, "I'd be glad to go out there with you. If you think there might be any trouble . . . ."

"No reason to think there'll be trouble. Anyway, I've put up with trouble all my life."

"I'm a fair to middlin' hand at speakin' Mexican. Better than Albert Stout, at least."

"Albert'll do. You stay here and watch out for Tommie."

Kelly nodded in resignation. Few people ever won an argument with Griffin Holliday. About the time it looked as if they might, Griff would go into a rage and it would be a fight instead of an argument. In a fight, nobody won over Griffin Holliday.

Kelly looked up the street, where the Barnhill buggy was turning a corner. "You said awhile back you might discharge Odom Willcox. I'm wonderin' why you don't."

Holliday shrugged. "Guess nobody better has come along. Anyway, the badge means so much to him. . . ."

"For the wrong reasons. You'll wish someday you'd done it."

"I'll get around to it, bye and bye." Holliday looked up at the morning sun. "It's a long ways out there. I'll miss my dinner." At his age many of life's other pleasures had faded, but one thing Griffin Holliday still enjoyed was a good meal.

Kelly grinned. "There's two or three ranches on that road. Somebody'd be glad to take you in and feed you."

"Might take a little *vuelta* by Frisco's headquarters. He's got an old Mexican woman doin' the cookin' for him. She can make a kitchen stove do anything but talk."

Presently another buggy came into sight. Driving it was a tall, angular man who belied his name, Albert Stout. He was probably Griff's best friend. He wore no badge, but Kelly knew it was the sheriff's practice to deputize him when he needed special help, especially if he needed an interpreter. Kelly had heard Stout talk Spanish. It wasn't really bad, but it was far from good. It was the kind of effort that made the Mexican kids cover their faces so people wouldn't see them laugh. Mostly Griff just liked Albert Stout's pleasant company and saw to it that Albert had a chance every so often to draw some county pay.

Albert saw Kelly and waved good-naturedly. "How's Tommie? She dominoed yet?"

Kelly shook his head. "Not yet."

"When she was little she used to take orders from me. You tell her I said hurry up."

Griff climbed into the buggy, straining a little at the effort. There had been a time he would simply have ridden a horse, but now a buggy was a lot more comfortable.

Well, Kelly thought, *after all these years a man is entitled.* He said, "You be careful now, Griff."

"I always been careful. How else do you think I've got this old?" Griff looked at Stout. "Get rollin', Albert. If we time it right, we'll make Frisco's headquarters for dinner."

Chacho and Felix had argued most of the way home. Now on the porch of the little frame house — shack, better called — the argument went on. Felix watched the sorrel mare, which stood unsaddled in the sagging old pen built long ago of mesquite trunks and branches. He took second wind for continuation of the disagreement.

"I say that once you saddled her and rode away from Barnhill's, you should never have taken the saddle off. You should have kept riding. You watch, *hermano*, they will be after you."

"She is mine. By all rights — by his promise — she is mine."

"You say she is yours, but you are a Mexican. Since when does a Mexican have anything to say about the law? They will be coming for you. If they do not kill you outright, they will at least take you away to prison. And Barnhill will get back his sorrel mare."

Not once had Felix suggested that Chacho simply take her back to Barnhill. He recognized that the damage was irreparably done the moment Chacho had struck the man. No matter what amends might be attempted, none would ever undo what had already been done.

"I say run, Chacho."

"Where would I go? This is home."

"This? Home?" Felix snorted. "It is not even our house. It all belongs to the old gringo Frisco."

29

"A good man."

"But still a gringo. I tell you, go to Mexico."

"I have never been in Mexico. This land is all I ever knew."

"You will feel at home in Mexico. It is something we have always carried here" — he tapped his chest with his finger — "even if we have never seen it. There you can be away from the gringo forever."

"There is hardship and injustice everywhere, even in Mexico. If that were not so, our grandfathers would not have left it."

"They did not leave it. All this was once a part of Mexico. The gringo came and took it. Our grandfathers chose to stay."

"I am too much of a man to run because one gringo lies and cheats."

"To the gringos you are no man at all. You are only a Mexican."

Felix was just like old man Esteban Bustamante, Chacho thought, seeing nothing except the bad in anyone whose eyes were blue and whose skin was pale. "The sheriff has always seemed to me to be a good man. And the patron, Mister Frisco, he will tell them my word is good."

For the twentieth time Felix called Chacho a fool. But they were brothers. A man might fight his brother every day of his life, but he would die for him should danger come at him from outside.

"If you are afraid to ride for Mexico alone, I will go with you."

Chacho frowned. From the shack he could hear Felix's chunky wife, Dolores, washing up the dishes from the noonday meal, humming some foolish little cantina ditty that no respectable woman was supposed to know. "What of *her*? You could not leave her."

"For a little while, only."

"She would not like it."

"She is but a woman. It is not for her to say what she likes and does not like."

"There is no need, *hermano*," Chacho said tightly. "I am a grown man; I could get to Mexico by myself, if I chose to go. Anyway, would they not expect me to run for Mexico? Is that not where all of our people try to go when trouble comes? If they wanted me they would spread out their posses like a net for fish, and they would not let me get to Mexico at all. If I were to want to run, I would fool them and go north from here."

30

"Because of that girl, that Luisa Aguilar? She lives to the north."

"The mare is hers."

"The mare is yours. You had better use her while you still have time. And south to Mexico, not north toward more gringos."

"North is where I would go if I ran. But I will not run!"

Felix looked off into the distance, and his jaw sagged in dismay. "No matter. Now it is too late to run."

Chacho turned, the bright afternoon sun pinching his eyes before he made out the vehicle coming up the narrow wagon road that wound like two tiny ribbons through the jungle of green mesquite. Few men ever came here except the landowner Frisco, and this was not Frisco's buggy.

"The *rinches*," Felix said darkly. "At the very least, the *cherife*." He pushed to his feet, his hands flexing nervously.

Chacho felt misgivings now that he faced up to the immediate reality; before, the idea of arrest had been something abstract, not quite real. He had told himself he could simply explain the truth of the matter and they would somehow believe him over the lies of the trader Barnhill. That had been while he was talking in the silence of his mind to an imaginary and understanding sheriff.

But that buggy was real, and so were the two men sitting in it. Now the palms of his hands began to sweat, and he rubbed them against his legs. Looking for something hopeful he said, "They must not think I am a very big thief. There is no posse; there are just two men."

"Two men are enough to kill you," Felix said, his voice edged with dread. He stepped into the house. Chacho heard Dolores gasp and cry out in protest. She was still crying when Felix returned to the high, narrow little porch. He held a pistol.

Chacho exclaimed, "Put it away. If they see that they will kill us."

On the porch lay Felix's big straw hat. He shoved the pistol under it, out of sight. "It is not for them to see. But if I am right and you are wrong, brother, we will need it."

The wagon road made a sharp turn around a large water-lot in which considerable herds of cattle were sometimes gathered, and then it made an almost-straight line for the unfenced house. As the buggy came out upon the straight stretch, Chacho recognized the sheriff slumped in the seat. The driver was a tall man, doubtless a deputy of some kind. It had long been his observation that the gringo lawmen did not often travel alone; they traveled in pairs, at least.

Chacho stepped down from the porch and moved out a few feet in front of the house. Behind him he could hear Felix coming down also, but Felix stopped short, within reach of the straw hat. The driver stopped the pair of bay horses and spoke to them in a slow, gentle voice. The horses seemed grateful for the pause and almost immediately went into a tired, three-legged stance.

The sheriff suspiciously eyed Chacho and Felix, each in his own turn, then let his gaze come to rest on Chacho. "You'd be the one they call Chacho?" he asked in English.

Chacho understood. "Si, *soy* Chacho Fernandez."

That much the sheriff also understood. But he turned to the tall man beside him. "Albert, I expect I better turn the real talkin' over to you. After I've said howdy I'm just about finished in Mexican."

Albert Stout repeated the sheriff's question, but Chacho didn't get a chance to answer. The sheriff waved his hand impatiently and said, "He already said he was; I understood that much." Griffin Holliday looked at the frame house, suspicion still showing. A question was plain in his eyes: *Wonder how many are in the house?*

In Spanish Chacho said, "There is no one in the house except the wife of my brother Felix."

Stout translated. Holliday studied Chacho and seemed to decide he was telling the truth. "Ask him if he knows who I am?"

Chacho volunteered that he knew the *cherife*, that he had spoken to him only this morning in town. He repeated what he had said on that occasion, that he had taken nothing except what belonged to him.

Stiffly, a little painfully, the sheriff climbed to the ground. He stretched himself, rubbing his hip which evidently hurt from the ride. He looked past the house toward the little shed which served for a barn, and toward the sorrel mare which had her head poked over the crude old fence; she was looking with interest at the buggy horses.

"Ask him if that is the mare he took from Barnhill?"

Chacho understood but delayed an answer, pondering just what to say as the tall man translated the question into a poor grade of Spanish, shamefully misusing several words. It occurred to Chacho that if the sheriff was paying this man for nothing more than to be an interpreter, the county was being cheated.

"This is the mare Barnhill promised me for breaking his broncs."

"That ain't the way Barnhill tells it. He says you were promised a different horse and that you took this one by force, that you beat him and left him for dead."

"Barnhill lies."

"I wouldn't be surprised. Somebody lies, that's for damn sure."

The way Albert Stout translated that, it came out that Chacho was lying. Chacho had understood enough of the sheriff's words to know that was not the way it was meant, but Felix knew no English. He knew what was being said only from the bad translations made by Stout. His face flushed, and his eyes began to snap in anger. Chacho held up his hand in a gesture for Felix to hold still.

"I do not lie, *Señor cherife*. There was no other horse, only this one. Barnhill said she would be mine. But when I went to get her he told me I could not have her. He tried to make me take a common mare you would not even give your children."

Albert Stout almost choked on that speech. He struggled and used the wrong words and corrected himself and managed to come out with a reasonable facsimile of what Chacho had said.

The sheriff's eyes bored into Chacho as if they were

33

exploring all his thoughts, all his secret sins that no one knew except himself and the priest who took confession. "I got a feelin', boy, that you're tellin' me the truth. But I can't take it that way on my own hook. I'll have to take you and the mare to town and let you and Barnhill stand up in front of a judge."

Much of that went over Chacho's head, and he had to wait for the translation. Stout said enough that Chacho understood that the sheriff was taking him and the mare back to town. For the first time he began to feel that Felix had been right all along; they were going to give the mare back to Barnhill and put Chacho in jail.

"No!" Chacho declared. "She is my mare. You don't take her."

The sheriff was a little startled by the show of resistance. Anger began to rise in his face. "I'll see that you get treated fair, but you got to come."

Chacho's stance turned stiff, and he could feel his heart beginning to pound. "No! You are not going to take her."

The sheriff was angry now. "Boy, I been tryin' to give you the benefit of the doubt. Now, dammit, if you don't come of your own accord I'm going' to have to arrest you!"

Chacho could feel the blood pulsing in his temples. "I have done nothing wrong. You can't arrest me for nothing."

Albert Stout made a fatal mistake in translation. Chacho used the Spanish word *nada*, for "nothing." But Stout mistook it for *nadie*, which meant "nobody."

34

Alarmed, he told the sheriff, "He says he ain't goin' to let nobody arrest him."

Thoroughly angered, the sheriff said, "The hell he ain't," and drew the pistol from his holster.

Afterward, Chacho would let the next few seconds run through his mind a thousand times, as if by doing so he could somehow change what happened. He knew instantly that Stout had given the wrong translation, but he was powerless to stop the events the deputy's mistake had set into motion.

Felix shouted, "He's going to kill you, Chacho!" and grabbed at the straw hat on the porch. Chacho saw the flash of movement and shouted, "No, Felix, don't!"

But Felix had the pistol in his hand and was swinging it at the sheriff. The sheriff, seeing him, spun halfway around on his heel and shifted his own pistol away from Chacho, toward Felix. Holliday's pistol roared. The impact flung Felix back against the porch. Dying, he pulled the trigger by reflex. His pistol kicked up dust at the sheriff's feet.

Chacho saw blood coming from his brother's mouth. He saw that the sheriff, numb from the shock of the moment, was about to fire again. Chacho grabbed the big man's wrist and pushed it up, making the second shot waste itself in the air. "No!" Chacho shouted. "Don't shoot him again; don't kill him!"

In a frenzy of excitement the sheriff tried to twist his arm free of Chacho's strong grip. Chacho got hold of the pistol barrel and pushed it away from himself. For a moment he and the sheriff stood shoving each other, cold sweat breaking out on both their faces, panic blocking Chacho's throat, cutting off his breath. He strained until he felt his eyes were going to pop out of his head as he tried to twist the pistol from the sheriff's grip. For an instant he thought he had it.

It went off then, a third time, blistering the hand that held the barrel. The sheriff fell away from him, crying out in shock and pain. Whatever hold Holliday had on the pistol, he relinquished, leaving it in Chacho's hands.

Chacho looked at those hands and found them bloody. He saw blood spilling out between the fingers the sheriff held tight against his broad belly. He saw the momentary look of dismay in the round face, the ashen gray that almost immediately replaced the angry red. The sheriff looked at him with accusing eyes and tried to speak, but the only sound which came from him was a groan. Then, like an old tree which has withstood the wind as long as it can but resists all the way to the ground, he slowly began to lean forward. He sprawled out on his face and lay gasping.

Chacho stood in a half crouch, the pistol still gripped awkwardly by the barrel though the heat was burning his fingers. He looked down at the fallen sheriff, unable to believe what he had done. He looked up then at the tall man in the buggy. Albert Stout's thin face seemed nothing but a pair of big eyes filled with horror. Stout stared at the dying sheriff, then slowly lifted his gaze to the pistol in Chacho's hands.

Chacho tried to say something to him, but the words stuck in his throat. Suddenly Stout came out of the trance. He made no move toward a gun; Chacho doubted afterward that he even had one. The two horses had been startled by the shots and danced in fear. Stout shouted at them and popped the whip and set them into a run. He had the whole space between the house and the corral fence to make a turn, and he used it. The buggy tilted up on two wheels, then righted itself.

Desperately Stout struggled to gain control of the horses as he raced the buggy away, back onto the road over which he had come. Chacho heard Dolores screaming at the top of her lungs as she came running down the steps and threw herself over the still form of her husband.

Chacho's hands came open finally, and the pistol fell to his feet. He half turned to look down on his fallen brother.

"Oh, God," he cried out. "God help us all!"

FOUR

Chacho knelt by his brother and took the outstretched hand, desperately looking for sign that life yet lingered. He pleaded to the saints and the Holy Mother Mary, but there was no pulse.

"Felix," he called huskily. "Felix!"

Felix was past hearing. The only sound was Dolores' crying. Chacho wiped a dusty sleeve across his burning eyes. His sight was still blurred by the hot flow of tears. He made no effort to stop himself. There was a time for holding in and a time for crying. Instinctively he knew there would soon be a time when he would have to hold in. He accepted release now, while he could still afford it.

He pushed up from his knees and staggered a few steps to drop again by the sheriff. Holliday lay on his back, choking in his own blood but too weak to help himself. Chacho turned him over on his side to give him what little relief he could.

"Why, *cherife?*" Chacho cried, the tears running hot

down his face. "Why did you do it? I did not want to hurt you."

Holliday might have heard him, but he was too far gone for any verbal response. He seemed to be trying to speak, but Chacho could make out only a thick-tongued murmuring. There was a word that might have been a woman's name . . . the sheriff's wife, perhaps. The murmuring stopped. The sheriff had gone off after Felix.

Chacho sat on the ground and covered his face in his arms, letting himself go for a little while. But gradually he became aware again of his sister-in-law and her anguish. The brothers had told her nothing that would prepare her for a thing like this. This unexpected, savage turn of events had struck her like a thunderbolt.

Chacho took her in his arms. He managed, after a bit, to get her to turn loose of Felix and rise to her feet. "Come over into the shade of the porch," he said gently, "and I'll bring Felix in out of the sun."

He seated Dolores on the bottom step. She sat there, staring in shock at the two dead men in the yard. Chacho picked up Felix's limp body, having to let the legs drag as he moved his brother to the shade and stretched him out on his back on the porch. Gradually he straightened the legs and folded Felix's arms. He pulled off Felix's boots. It was not good for a man to die with his boots on. Felix was already dead, but the gesture had to be made. Chacho kissed his brother on the forehead and crossed himself.

Dolores sat on the steps and sobbed, but now for Chacho the time for crying was over. He had to think and think fast. He blinked away the vestige of tears and tried to see what had become of the man in the buggy. He could hear him far away, still shouting at the horses.

Chacho began to perceive the desperate trouble he was in. He began to calculate how long it would take for the man to reach help. Probably the nearest place — depending upon which direction he took — would be the Frisco headquarters. That would take him fully half an hour if he ran the horses all the way, which he probably would. The return would take another half an hour, even if he found someone at the headquarters ready to turn around with him and come back immediately. An hour then, at the least, before anyone got here.

But to accept that as a certainty was to overlook the possibility of bad luck, and Chacho had had plenty of bad luck already today. There was always a chance the man in the buggy might run into someone along the road before he ever reached the Frisco place. In such a case he could be back in much less than an hour.

And God, what a story he was likely to tell. . . . The way the tall man had looked as he had wheeled that buggy around and had whipped the horses away from here in a run.

Whoever came back with him now would come looking for the worst. They would come with guns cocked and ready, and they would shoot anything that moved.

A sense of urgency took hold of Chacho, pushing aside his grief. "Dolores, we have to get away from here, both of us."

If she heard, she gave no sign of it. He put his arm around her shoulder and told her again. This time she shook her head. "This is my home; my Felix is here. I do not want to go anywhere."

"But there will be much trouble. We have killed a sheriff."

"You have killed a sheriff. I have done nothing."

"There will be men here after a while, angry and desperate. They will hurt whoever they find here, even you. They will not ask whether you had any part in this. They will only know that you are one of us."

She was still in shock and did not comprehend. "I am not going."

Chacho could not afford the time to argue with her. He would have to take her whether she wanted to go or not. He looked toward the corrals, his gaze fastening on the sorrel mare. His eyes hardened. He walked over and picked up the fallen pistol near the sheriff's body. He rubbed some of the dirt from it onto his old trousers and strode in stiff, measured steps toward the corral gate. He swung the gate open and stood in the narrow opening, the pistol down at arm's length. The horses were still skittish from the shooting and shied away from him. They turned at the far end of the pen, their suspicious ears pointed at him.

Chacho stared at the mare, then deliberately raised the pistol. "You were the cause of this," he said bitterly. "You are not worth the lives of two men."

She stood looking at him, still nervous and apprehensive. Chacho's hand tightened on the pistol as he brought the sights into line. But his hand trembled; he could not hold it steady. He lowered the pistol a little, thinking if he rested his arm a moment it would be better. He raised the pistol again. Not only was his hand trembling, but his eyes were blurring.

"Damn you, *maqui*, why don't you hold still?"

She was holding perfectly still; it was Chacho who could not be steady. He tried in vain to take a bead and hold it. Each time he was close, the tears came again. He lowered the pistol, knowing he could not use it.

"*Maqui*," he admitted, "the fault was not yours; it was mine."

For a wild moment, knowing the enormity of his trouble, he felt a strong impulse to raise the pistol to his own head and escape the hell that awaited him. But he had listened much to the priests as a boy, and though he seldom saw the inside of a church any more the training was still with him. To murder himself was unthinkable. He stuck the pistol in his waistband.

He went to his saddle and got his maguey rope. He shook out a loop and sailed it over the head of Felix's horse. That one, he thought, would be gentle enough for Dolores. She would have to ride Felix's saddle, astride; there was no sidesaddle for her. Sidesaddles were mostly for gringo women anyhow, or for the high-bred wives of the Spanish *gachupines* who regarded themselves as being far above the common folk. Chacho threw Felix's big-horned saddle on the horse and tightened the cinch.

He shook out another loop and looked at the pretty sorrel mare. "Little *maqui*," he said darkly, "we have many hard miles ahead of us, you and I. We will pay dearly for what has happened here." He swung the loop. Once caught, she came to him without hesitation, though her ears were alert, her eyes watchful. He saddled her and led the two horses out the gate, leaving it open. There was no need for shutting it; he knew he could never come back here.

He led the horses to the little frame house. He wasted a minute or so in looking at it, regretting leaving it. It was typical of the structures the Anglo ranchers built on these places for the use of their renters or help. If a Mexican had built it, it would have been of adobe or stone, low of roof and resting solidly upon the ground, its floor of the ageless earth. It would have been warmer in winter and cooler in summer. But the Anglo had an aversion to living on the ground; he seemed to feel it demeaned him somehow, so he liked to stand above and apart from the good Mother Earth.

Chacho had liked this place, though the cold winter wind sometimes whistled through the clapboard siding and sought its way to a man's bones, even when he stood near enough to the stove to blister his brown hide. And in summer the thin walls seemed only to trap the sun's heat and hold it in. He had liked the old man Frisco, who believed that a Mexican must always be kept busy to prevent him from getting lazy but was never petty or mean about it. He paid an honest wage and never chiseled on the groceries he agreed to furnish. Chacho and Felix had lived here a year before Felix had married Dolores. That event had forced Chacho to begin sleeping under the shed. It was worth that sacrifice to have a woman to do the cooking.

He led the horse to Dolores. "Come. I will help you mount."

She blinked. "I am not going."

"You are not staying here. I will take you to your relatives. You can stay there until the worst has passed."

She cried again. "I do not want to leave Felix."

"Felix has left us both. If we do not get away from here we may follow him. Come on. I do not want to carry you."

Still she sat there, unmoving, and for an impatient moment Chacho was reminded that Felix had chosen his wife for her cooking and not for superior intelligence. He grabbed her beneath the arms and lifted her up. She protested, more surprised than angry.

"I have things in the house," she said. "I cannot leave my things."

"You have nothing that is worth more than your life." He half-lifted her onto the horse, her skirts pushing far up her legs. Her feet barely touched the tops of the stirrups. But there was no time now to unlace the stirrup leathers and readjust them to fit her. She would have to do the best she could and hold onto the horn if necessary; it was large enough for both of her hands.

The tears rolled down her cheeks. "We cannot leave Felix like this."

"Someone will bury Felix. We must see to it that they do not also bury us." He swung onto the sorrel mare, which seemed ready and eager. That ride out from town this morning had not taxed her much. But Chacho wondered and worried a little about the horse Dolores was on; it had been to town and back today, with only a short rest since.

He spurred out of the yard in a trot, trying not to look back but unable to help himself. He knew that as long as he lived he would never forget the terrible sight that lay behind him . . . two men killed in a senseless moment for a senseless cause . . . for another man's faithless promise, and for that man's greed. Chacho shut his eyes to the sudden resumption of blinding tears, and he turned his head away. Dolores followed after him, sobbing again.

A chill gripped him, a chill that led gradually to an over-all numbness. He moved into a lope, angling somewhat to the south but also a little westward. He could hear Dolores' horse coming behind him, and he didn't look back. If he looked back he might have to see once more what he was leaving behind, and he didn't think he could stand that again.

He had no plan. He tried now to begin thinking ahead, but his mind kept running back to those violent moments in the yard. He relived them in terrible detail a hundred times.

He mustered enough will finally to put it away from him, at least for a while. He began projecting himself into the future, trying to guess what the gringo law would do and how he could counter them. He had never had the law hot on his trail before, not even those times he had helped relay horses south to the river. But he had known men who did. Some got away, some didn't. Those who didn't were likely to die wherever they were found. The old Mexican custom of *ley fuga* — shooting the fugitive — was readily accepted on both sides of the border. It was safer to those doing the hunting, and simpler than bringing a man in alive. There were no lawyers to wrangle with, no appeal that might set a guilty man free. And there was never any doubt about a fugitive's guilt; he had run, hadn't he?

To Chacho's recollection just about every Mexican he ever heard of who got in bad trouble in Texas had run south, trying to reach the Rio Grande and the sanctuary of Mexico. It made sense now for him to do the same. Rarely was a man ever offered up out of Mexico for some crime committed in Texas unless that crime had been a particularly heinous one, and perpetrated against another Mexican. A man who killed a *cherife* or a *rinche* was safe if he ever made the river. He was likely even to be regarded as a hero of sorts, for a state of mutual antagonism still remained between *la raza* and the gringo, an angry heritage going back through all the border wars to the fall of the Alamo and even before. There had been provocation enough on both sides to justify a lifetime of hostility. That hostility now was beginning to fade, but its death was slow and painful.

Chacho had no wish to go to Mexico. He had never been there, not into the country proper. This was his home, not that tired old land of his forefathers. Moreover, every *rinche* from here to the river would expect him to run south, and they would be watching. Getting through them would be a challenge even to a man used to riding the back trails in the darkness. Chacho did not know if he had that keen coyote instinct that meant survival. He would have a hard time fooling all those *cherifes.*

Bueno, if they expected him to go south, he would do the opposite. North was where he had rather go anyway, north to the country where Luisa Aguilar lived. Maybe when he got up there old Esteban Bustamante could advise him. The old man had friends and relatives in the region of San Antonio. A Mexican could easily lose himself because so many of his own kind lived there, and the gringo law could hardly tell one from another. If a man's name was Pedro Duran and he said it was Juan Sanchez, then to the law he was Juan Sanchez; all Mexicans looked alike.

After a time the law would stop searching for him, sure he had made it to Mexico. And if any of the Mexican people in and around Domingo ever learned his whereabouts they would never talk. They kept a code of silence for mutual protection except when the crime was outrageous not only in gringo eyes but in their own.

Chacho's first problem would be in convincing the law that he had gone south. He and Dolores were traveling the right direction now for it. They would reach Sancho Creek in about three miles more. It still flowed heavily at this early season of year. That creek began to dwell on Chacho's mind. He knew within reason that sooner or later a dozen heavily armed men would be following his trail as fast as they could travel without losing sight of the track. By the time they followed it to the creek there would be no doubt in their minds that Chacho and the woman were on their way to Mexico.

Dolores began to complain. "We are going too fast. This horse is pounding the life out of me."

"Better him than a bullet," Chacho said, dismissing her objection without another moment's thought.

"I want to go back," she cried.

Chacho gave her a hard glance and started to say something cruel. But he caught himself; nothing that had happened had been her fault. His, perhaps, but not hers. "Stay with me," he said, deliberately holding his voice down.

After a time they reached the creek at a place Chacho knew well. He reined the sorrel mare to a stop and spent a minute or two looking at the water, and at the bank on the far side. Here the bank was sandy and they would leave deep tracks just at the water's edge. A little downstream, on a bend, he knew of a gravel bar left by past years' flooding, when the velocity of the water was slowed by the shift in direction. He studied a bit, trying to decide how he might use that gravel bar to advantage.

He didn't want to ride into the creek and turn abruptly upstream. If the *rinches* found no tracks leading out on the other side they would suspect what he had done. But how to leave some tracks over there, then get back into the water without showing it?

That was where the gravel bar might be useful.

"You stay here a minute," he told Dolores. He rode off into the water and moved the horse downstream in the center of it. He stood in his stirrups, trying to see over the opposite bank without climbing up on it. Presently he was satisfied. He rode back upstream to where Dolores waited. Her head was down, and her cheeks were wet again.

He beckoned to her to ride into the creek with him. She was slow to move but finally edged the horse down into the water just before Chacho decided to ride up and get her. He was not sure whether to pity her or to strike her. To strike a woman was not necessarily a bad thing, he thought; sometimes it was a good way to get her attention. But he deferred to Dolores' grief.

"Give me your bridle reins," he said holding out his hand. "I will lead your horse where I want him to go."

Silently she complied. She hadn't used the reins much anyway; her horse had simply followed Chacho's mare.

Taking the reins, Chacho led the way up a smooth part of the bank and out on the other side. Looking back, he saw that their tracks had been left deep in the mud at the creek's edge; some were already filling up with water. A blind gringo riding in the dark could not miss those. Chacho rode up onto more level ground, then angled southwestward, following fairly closely to the creek. In a few minutes he came to the gravel bar. At the far edge of it, a dozen or so loose horses and mules were standing, either watering or having watered. They wore the Frisco brand. Chacho rode onto the thick gravel, leading Dolores' mount and looking back to see if the hoofs were leaving any visible trace. He could see none.

"God is with us," he said. He took off his hat and waved it, shouting. The loose horses shied away from him as he hoped they would. They struck out away from the creek in a long trot.

Chacho said in satisfaction, "They will leave enough tracks now to set those gringos on half a dozen false trails. Now, sister, back into the water." Staying on the gravel, he led her horse into the creek and turned upstream again.

Dolores did not understand. "We already came this way. Why are we back in the water again? I don't like the water."

It surprised him that she didn't realize what he had been doing, or why. "We don't leave any tracks in this creek."

"I don't like the water," she complained again.

He didn't look at her. He kept riding, leading her horse.

The sorrel mare didn't particularly like the water either, and it took firmness on his part to keep her from moving up onto one bank or the other. Finally she became resigned to the idea and walked along in the middle of the creek without resistance to him. He looked back often, worrying over the way their movement muddied the shallow water.

Presently Dolores began sobbing again. It was not enough for a woman to be a good cook, Chacho thought. She ought to have some backbone, too. He questioned what had possessed his brother to marry such a one, though of course he had never had occasion to know the passionate side of her nature. He compared her to Luisa Aguilar and found her wanting on every count.

A pity.

46

FIVE

ommie had awakened soon after her father left with
Albert Stout in the buggy. Kelly Sadler had an affection-
ate reunion with his wife while her mother thoughtfully
left the house and went somewhere to borrow some
sugar. Rummaging around in the kitchen for a cup to
pour some coffee in, Kelly found that Mrs. Holliday already
had a sackful of sugar in the pantry. He was lucky in his choice
of mother-in-law; he knew men who were not so nobly blessed.

Tommie brought his hand up to her face and held it
tightly against her cheek. "I've missed you, Kelly. I wish I
were home."

"You are home."

"This used to be home, but not any more. Home is
where you are."

"I'll take you home soon as the baby comes and the doctor says you're able. Sure you're feelin' all right?"

"Fine." She smiled and kissed his hand. "But I feel better now."

Kelly didn't hold her as tightly as he wanted to; that would stir up hungers he could do nothing about. As far as that was concerned, Mrs. Holliday could just as well have stayed here. But he appreciated the spell of privacy.

Much later he was back on the front porch again; he always felt underfoot in a house when women were working. He fidgeted for something to do to occupy his time. Idleness was not a comfortable state for him. But Griffin Holliday had no cow to feed and milk, no garden to hoe. Such things might have gotten in his way as sheriff sometimes.

Kelly watched the sporadic movement of traffic up and down the dirt street . . . horseback riders, wagons, hacks, Mexican burros. Joe Florey passed by once in his wagon, hauling a short load of lumber. He gave the porch a quick glance, saw that Griffin Holliday wasn't on it and turned his head away. It was as if the old former Ranger had not seen Kelly Sadler at all.

I reckon a man sees what he wants to, and Joe sure don't want to see me, Kelly thought dourly. He could understand the old man's viewpoint, but it irritated him a little. Joe Florey had always been one to preach about the necessity of a man doing his duty. Looked like he could see that was all Kelly did when he said he thought it would be better for all concerned if Joe retired. Well, it was always easier to preach than to live up to the preaching.

He knew something was wrong when he saw the buggy turn a corner two blocks down the street. Even at the distance Kelly sensed that it was the one Griff and Albert Stout had been in. He jumped to his feet. The way the horses labored, he knew they had been run hard. As they came closer he could see the lather, the gleam of sweat shining in the sun. And he could see that Albert was in the buggy alone. Kelly was rushing through the gate when Albert sawed the lines and brought the horses to a halt. They stood heaving, their mouths open, their hides wet as if they had been caught in a rain.

He heard a screen door slam and heard the quick footsteps of Mrs. Holliday, rushing down the path behind him. He glanced back and saw Tommie on the porch, leaning against a post, fear in her paling face.

Stout was so excited he could hardly bring himself to speak. "Kelly . . . Kelly, I got to talk to you." He gave Mrs. Holliday a worried glance. "Kelly, I want to talk to you alone."

Mrs. Holliday's voice was strained. "Albert, where is my husband?"

Stout looked at Kelly, his eyes pleading. Kelly turned and took his mother-in-law by the arm. "Mother, it's best you go back up to the porch with Tommie."

She wasn't going. She looked straight at Albert Stout and demanded, "Albert . . . where did you leave my husband?"

Stout stammered. "Goddammit, Kelly, I can't. . . . I just can't tell it with them women here."

Mrs. Holliday screamed, "Tell me, Albert! Where's Griffin?"

Somehow, Kelly knew. And he was sure Mrs. Holliday knew; he could see the awful conviction in her eyes. Stunned, he said, "You better tell us, Albert."

Albert Stout was on the verge of crying. "They killed the best friend I ever had, Kelly. Them damn Meskins, they shot him dead!"

Mrs. Holliday cried out, and Kelly caught her in his arms as she seemed to slump forward. From the porch Tommie screamed, "Mother! Kelly! What's happened out there?"

Kelly tried to wave her back, but she came awkwardly down off the porch, trying to hurry. He was afraid she would fall, but he had his hands full holding Mrs. Holliday. Tears streamed down Tommie's face as she reached her husband, "Kelly, what's happened to Papa?"

The question was needless; she could tell from the men's faces and from her mother's sobbing. Then Kelly was holding two women, wishing he knew what in hell to say.

To talk brought knifing pain to his tight throat. "You real sure, Albert? You sure you didn't just run off and leave him out there?"

Stout vigorously shook his head. "I wisht I could say different, Kelly, but he's dead. I was there; I seen it."

"They ambushed him?"

Stout let it all spill out in an excited rush. "No, I reckon you'd have to say that Griff taken the first shot. He killed one of them Meskins. But that other one, he shot and killed Griff. He'd've shot me too, only I turned this buggy round and got the hell away from there. He was goin' to kill me, too, Kelly, I swear it. Otherwise I wouldn't've run. I didn't have no gun . . . wasn't expectin' to have no need for it. I couldn't stay there and let him kill me. Wouldn't've been no use, Griff already dead and all." Stout began to sob. "You think folks'll blame, me, Kelly? You reckon they'll call me a coward?" The thought must have haunted him on the way to town.

Kelly shook his head. "If Griff was dead, you did the only thing a man could do, Albert. You did right."

Tears rolled down Stout's sun-browned cheeks and into his stubble of graying whiskers. "Thanks, Kelly. I hoped you'd see it."

"You told anybody else yet?"

"No. I come by the Frisco headquarters. Wasn't a soul there but a couple of Mexican women. They went into a cryin' fit and wasn't no help at all. I come on to town as hard as the horses could run."

Kelly tried to think, to begin to evolve some plan. It was difficult, both of his arms full of crying women, his own eyes burning as if afire. "Albert, you reckon you can find Odom Willcox?" The thought of turning this problem over to Odom Willcox repelled Kelly, but Willcox had been Griffin Holliday's chief deputy; he was, in effect, sheriff now, pending action by the commissioners court for an election.

Odom Willcox, sheriff! The thought was bitter as alkali water.

"I'll find him," Stout vowed. "I'll find everybody. I'll bet half the town will be ready to ride out there in a few minutes. You want me to get a horse for you, Kelly?"

"I'd be obliged if you'd get me that good stout dun of Griff's. He's fresh, and he'll go to hell and back if he needs to."

"I'll bring him, Kelly."

The thought of a big mob rushing out yonder began to build dread in him. "Albert," he said, "it'd be better if you didn't spread word of this too fast. Just tell Odom and let him tell four or five others that he wants to have go along. We don't want. . . ."

The words were wasted. Albert Stout was gone, popping his whip over the half-dead animals, shouting at them, pushing them beyond endurance. They would be fortunate if they ever recovered.

Kelly tried again to project himself forward, to begin working on some kind of plan. But he could not think beyond the two distraught women. Neighbors converged in a run, sensing trouble by Albert Stout's excited actions, by the way Kelly was holding his wife and his mother-in-law. The neighbor women were shouting at other people, unseen inside houses or coming down the street.

Good God, Kelly thought helplessly, *the whole town'll know in ten minutes.*

To his gratification the women asked no foolish questions. They came to help. Because of them, he was able to get Tommie and Mrs. Holliday into the house. A couple of anxious neighbors escorted his mother-in-law into the back room and got her to lie down on the bed she would never share again with Griffin Holliday. Tommie sank into a rocking chair and sat there with her shoulders hunched; she rocked silently, holding back the tears that had flowed freely for a time outside. She looked at Kelly with eyes pinched in pain. "You goin' out there, Kelly?"

He nodded grimly. "It's my place to go. Not only as a Ranger, but because he was your father."

"I don't want you to."

"I have to. It's my place."

She nodded in resignation, crushing a handkerchief in her small hands. "Then be careful, Kelly. I don't want to

51

lose you too." She held the handkerchief to her mouth, and Kelly had a momentary fear that she was going to faint. But she didn't. Instead her voice took on a hardness he had never heard, an inheritance from old Griff that came out under stress. "If you have to go, then, do it right. Stay on his trail till you get him."

He leaned to her and took her hands. "I don't have any idea how long that'll be. You may have to get through the funeral without me. You may have that baby before I can get back."

"It's all right. I'll be here whenever you do come. Don't worry about me. Don't worry about anything but gettin' the man that killed Papa."

He looked up into the face of a middle-aged woman who lived across the street; be damned if he could remember her name. "You folks'll watch out over her?"

The woman nodded severely. "You go do your duty, Mister Sadler. We'll be here and do ours."

"I'm grateful to you, ma'am." Reluctantly he turned from Tommie and went into the bedroom they would have shared had he been here for the night. Draped across the back of a chair was his gunbelt, his pistol in the holster. He strapped on the belt and buckled it, picked up his spurs from the floor and methodically put them on. Through the window he saw men beginning to gather on horseback, talking loudly, angrily, many carrying rifles and shotguns.

God, he told himself dismally, *it's going to be worse than I thought.* He considered it probable that these possemen had more to fear from each other than from any Mexican horsethief. But how could a man send them home? Even if Kelly had the authority, Griffin Holliday had been a friend of every man here, more than likely. They had hired him to do for them the peace-keeping job which was his specialty. He had died in the performance of that duty. Now it was their duty, as they saw it, to see that his death did not go unpunished inasmuch as it had been suffered in their behalf. It was the way men thought in that time and place.

52

Kelly rough-counted fifteen or sixteen men. At another time there probably would be far more, but many townsmen were scattered in their individual lines of work; it would take time for the word to spread.

No matter; there were more than enough already.

Kelly noted sourly that the horse-trader Barnhill was among the men. Evidently he had not been hurt as badly as he had made out. It came to Kelly that if it had not been for Barnhill, Griffin Holliday even now would be sitting on that front porch taking his ease. He remembered that Griff had doubted Barnhill. Perhaps the fact that Griff was dead gave more weight to Barnhill's story.

The men milled in feverish expectancy. All turned to look as Odom Willcox hurried down the street, the deputy badge shining on his vest, a saddlegun held lightly in his left hand and balanced across his saddle. He seemed pleased at the size of the gathering.

A short distance behind came Albert Stout, his long legs extending well below the belly of a dappled gray horse. He led Griffin Holliday's good dun, with Kelly's saddle on its back. Kelly always carried his saddle along, even when he rode the stagecoach. He had had it dropped off at the wagonyard in case he wanted to use it. Kelly walked out and took the reins, nodding his thanks. He checked the cinch, knowing it was tight enough but feeling compelled to look anyway. It was against all his upbringing to have someone else saddle or unsaddle a horse for him; that was a thing a man did for himself.

Willcox pushed his horse up as Kelly swung into the saddle. "You figurin' to lead this posse, Kelly?"

Kelly frowned. "You want me to?"

"I thought you might want to, seein' as Griff was your papa-in-law. On the other hand, it ain't your county, and it is mine."

If Willcox was trying not to appear anxious, he was doing a poor job. It was written all over him that he wanted the honor of leading these men. If he had taken time to think about it — and Kelly suspected he had — he was already figuring how to change that deputy's badge for one that said *sheriff.*

Damn poor substitute for a good man, Kelly thought darkly. *I don't have to live here.*

He told Willcox, "They're your people. I'll just follow along."

Willcox nodded, accepting what he thought was only right. "You puttin' yourself under my orders too, Kelly?"

Kelly frowned. He hadn't thought of that. He sidestepped from making a promise. "When I can't follow you, I'll go another way."

"I appreciate it." Willcox turned in the saddle. "Everybody ready?"

They were, and Willcox set out in a hard trot. In a moment, though, Kelly heard a shout from behind them and glanced back, reining up. Down the street came a man waving his hand, loping a big black horse. Kelly knew those thin, slightly pinched shoulders. He said loudly, "Joe Florey's tryin' to catch up."

Odom Willcox didn't stop, but he pulled his horse to one side so he could see past the men who followed him. "Damned old man," he said impatiently, "why don't he stay home where he belongs?"

Someone spoke up. "We ought to wait for him, Odom. He's been a good officer in his day."

"But his day has been over with for a long time," Willcox replied sharply. "He'll get in the way."

Kelly said, "I'll watch out for him."

"He won't even speak to you."

"He doesn't have to. I'll still watch out for him."

Willcox reluctantly stopped, and the rest of the men did likewise, waiting for Joe Florey to catch up. Florey slowed the black as he neared the posse. He looked angry. "Why didn't somebody come tell me?" he demanded. "I had to hear it from a Mexican errand boy." He didn't even glance at Kelly.

Willcox said, "We figure we're apt to have a long, hard ride, Joe. The man that killed Griff, he's probably took out for Mexico. No tellin' how far we'll have to follow before we catch up and get him. Liable to be a tough trip, even for a young man."

Florey took a critical look at the riders and their accouterments. "Don't look to me like anybody come very well prepared, then. I don't see even a blanket, hardly, much less anything to eat."

"We'll just have to take grub where and when we find it," Willcox said. "Same way with sleep. If I was you, Joe, I'd go home and set down on my porch and rest myself."

"You ain't me," Florey replied stubbornly. "And I'll still be ahorseback when you've caved in under a bush. I've chased Indians farther than you've ever rode a train."

"Them Indians you chased are all old men now, the ones that lived. They're all layin' up in the shade of a tepee."

Florey's eyes narrowed. "Griff was one of the best friends I ever had. I'm goin' whether you like it or not."

"Now, Joe, I'm tryin' to be nice to you."

Kelly decided it was time to horn in. "Let him alone, Odom. I'll take the responsibility for Joe."

He caught a hard glance from both men. Joe Florey said, "I don't need you to stand up for me. I always took care of my own problems."

Kelly shrugged. "I was just thinkin' that you're still the best tracker that ever was."

Florey studied him with sharp eyes, looking for sign that Kelly was patronizing him. "You're damn right I am! I may be older than the rest of this crew, but I'm still as good a man as any of you. Better!"

Odom Willcox made a shallow effort to stare the old man down, but it was no contest. The deputy shrugged and looked at Kelly. "If you'll take the responsibility. . . ."

Kelly only nodded, not wanting to see Tracker Joe stirred any worse than he already was.

He knew more or less what to expect when they rode into the yard in front of the Mexican shack on the Frisco place, but he was not quite prepared for the shock of seeing Griffin

55

Holliday dead. He saw Joe Florey take one pained look and pull aside, out of the midst of the milling possemen.

Odom Willcox and three or four others trooped up onto the little porch, glancing down warily at the dead Mexican who lay there, arms folded peacefully across his chest. Willcox kicked the door open and jumped inside with his rifle thrust forward. Kelly figured it was for show; Willcox knew there wouldn't be anybody in there. The deputy came out carrying the rifle at arm's length and paused to look at the body of Felix Fernandez.

"Well, at least old Griff got one of them. Damn pity he didn't get them all, but I suppose that's what happens when a man stays in office till he's too old to do the job."

Kelly angered at the implied criticism of Griffin Holliday, and he cut a glance at Joe Florey. Florey had heard. He muttered to himself and went on about what he was doing, leading his horse in a broad circle, studying the ground for tracks.

Kelly walked out to him. "Findin' anything?"

Florey grunted, and Kelly didn't think the old man intended to answer him. But directly Florey said, "If there was any tracks we needed in the yard, them amateurs has already blotted them out, scratchin' around like a bunch of chickens."

Kelly shrugged. "I doubt there's anything over there that you need, Joe. What've you found?"

Florey pointed with his chin, south and a little west.. "Two horses. They taken out yonderway."

"Two? I sort of gathered by what Albert said that there-wasn't but one man left."

"One man, one woman." Florey seemed to be debating with himself over whether to tell anything more. But he did. "I seen a woman's footprint where she got on a horse. Wife to the one that got away, I reckon, or to the one layin' over yonder."

Kelly knelt to look at the tracks. "Which horse is the man ridin'?"

Florey pointed to a set of tracks slightly smaller than the

other. "That one. Normally I'd figure the man to be on the bigger horse, but that ain't the way it worked this time."

Kelly remembered the sorrel mare he had seen Chacho Fernandez riding as he and his brother left town after their encounter with the trader Barnhill. He raised up, looking for Barnhill. He motioned to the man and said, "Come over here for a minute." Normally he would have added *please*, but not for Barnhill. Griff hadn't liked the man, and Kelly had great respect for Griff's ability to judge character.

Barnhill was standing afoot but swung onto his horse for the short distance rather than walk and lead. Kelly pointed to the tracks. "You recognize either set as bein' from that sorrel mare?"

Barnhill got down and frowned over the tracks, finally settling to his knees. He pointed to the smaller set. "That's the ones."

"You sure?"

"I know my own horses. I know their tracks." He clenched his fist. "Damn Mexican is tryin' to run off to Mexico with my mare."

Kelly frowned. "Seems to me like there was some question just whose mare she was. Griff was still in doubt when he left town."

Barnhill jerked his head toward the figure which someone now had covered with a blanket. "Looks like he found out." He said it with some hint of satisfaction, as if Holliday had received a just retribution for ever having doubted Barnhill's word. "I get the chance, I'll kill that horse-stealin' Mexican."

Kelly's voice drew tight. "For stealin' your horse, or for killin' Griffin Holliday?"

"I just come to do my duty, like every man here."

Kelly pointed his chin toward the yard. "You know he died for you."

"He died doin' a job the county paid him for. Just happened it was my trouble he was seein' about when it happened to him. Another day it could've been somebody else's. He knew the risks when he taken the job."

"I'm just hopin' he didn't die for nothin'."

Barnhill felt compelled to continue defending his story. "I had that mare as good as sold to a man from San Antonio for two hundred dollars. That Mexican stole her, just like I told Griff."

The more Barnhill talked, the more Kelly wondered. But he said, "All right. I just hope I never find out different."

"You won't."

It had been a long ride from town, and Odom Willcox suggested it would be a good idea for the men to fix themselves something to eat here, and get some hot coffee. There was a sack of coffeebeans in the kitchen, and a few canned goods, and about half of a skinned goat hanging out back, wrapped in a piece of bloodstained tarp. Somebody rolled the dead Mexican off of the porch and onto the ground to make room, covering him up with an old blanket so nobody would have to look at him. Griffin's body had been moved in against the side of the house, out of the sun.

While this was going on, Willcox surveyed with satisfaction what Joe Florey was doing. Quietly, in as few words as could be used to say it all, Florey told him what he had found. Willcox nodded confidently, looking in the direction where the tracks went. "Mexico. That's what I figured all the time."

Kelly nodded silently. It was a logical guess. Any three-year-old boy could have made it under the circumstances.

Willcox said, "I'll send Albert back in to get on the telephone and alert everybody to the south of us. With us pushin' on him from behind, and every law officer to the south waitin' to pick him up, that chili won't have the chance of a three-legged jackrabbit in a wolf den." He looked thoughtfully at Florey. "It'd be a good idea all around if you'd go back in with Albert. You could help him on the telephone . . . get the word to Ranger headquarters in Austin and let them contact everybody south of here."

It was a transparent effort. Joe Florey's eyes weren't that bad. "Send somebody else with Albert. I'm goin' on."

Willcox shrugged. "Suit yourself. We'll have us a bite to eat, then we'll set out followin' them tracks."

Florey straightened. "This bunch? All they'll do is wipe

out the tracks, like they've already done around the yard.
You and them couldn't follow a spotted elephant through
short grass. I'm goin' on ahead while the trail is still clear.
You all stay behind me so you don't mess it up."

He didn't make it as a suggestion; he said it as a com-
mand. It set Willcox back a little. The deputy rubbed his
chin, picking around carefully for the words so he wouldn't
suffer another bite from this sharp-tongued old man. "Joe,
I got all the confidence in the world in you, but there's
some of the boys may think your eyes. . . ."

"I can see better with my eyes *shut* than this bunch could
see with a pair of binoculars. You keep them behind me,
Odom, you hear that? Don't you let them be messin' up
the trail till I'm done with it."

Florey swung into the saddle. Willcox asked, "Ain't you
goin' to eat?"

"I already et once today. It don't take much for an old
man."

Kelly came near smiling at the way Joe walked over
Willcox. The deputy had never had occasion to learn that
old Joe Florey's bite was even worse than his bark. "You
better leave well enough alone, Odom," Kelly said when
the old man had gone beyond hearing. "When he makes
his mind up, nothin' will change him, not man nor beast."

Kelly mounted Griffin Holliday's dun and started to follow Florey. The old man soon became conscious of him
and halted, turning in the saddle, his eyes sharp and angry.
He squinted a little, evidently having trouble at first making
out just who Kelly was. "Oh, it's you. Thought you heard
what I told Odom."

"I heard."

"Then go on back. All you spectators do is to ruin the
trail."

"You know me better than that. I'll stay and keep an eye
out for you. You can't study tracks and watch for ambush
at the same time."

It was a common practice among Rangers to send a man
along to protect the tracker so he could apply his full atten-

tion to the job and not have to worry about somebody catching him unaware. Several times Kelly had provided that function for Joe Florey when Florey was called upon to follow a dfficult trail.

"My eyes are all right," Florey said defensively.

"Still, it's better to have four good eyes than two."

The old Ranger knew the logic of Kelly's argument but could not bring himself to acknowledge it. He had rather be sided by almost anyone else. Kelly considered a little more gentle persuasion, then thought *the hell with it!* It was time he met the old man's hostility head-on.

"Joe, you think I was wrong about you. All right then, let's see you prove it to me."

Florey looked him squarely in the eyes, ungiving. "It'd pleasure this old heart of mine to see you admit you made a mistake. If you're man enough. . . ."

"You prove it and we'll see what kind of man I am."

Florey accepted the challenge with a curt nod. "All right then, you tend to your job and I'll do mine. But you let some son of a bitch shoot me and I'll shoot you before I cash in."

"Fair enough."

Older men who remembered Joe Florey from his younger days said he had always been cranky and demanding, and he had become even more so in his later years. *Give him another twenty years,* Kelly thought, *and there won't nobody be able to live within a mile of him.* Pity a good man like that had to get old. Even more painful when he couldn't recognize it.

Florey turned back to the task at hand. The tracks at this point were easy, and he moved along in a brisk trot. Florey rode on the left-hand side of the tracks because it was more natural for him to lean to his right, looking down. Kelly stayed on the other side, careful never to let his horse cross over the tracks and obscure them in any way. A man never knew, in a job like this, when he might have to ride back a ways and start over on some segment of a trail.

SIX

No one asked foolish questions at the small farmhouse where Dolores' aunt and uncle lived. The two old people had seen Chacho and Dolores coming from afar and had sensed from the way they rode that something was terribly wrong. The uncle, *Tio* Benito, walked out to meet them. He said simply, "I do not see Felix." It was a way of posing a question without actually asking one.

Chacho told him what he had somehow known he would hear. "Felix is dead. I have brought Dolores home to stay with you."

Benito helped Dolores down from the horse, and *Tia* Serafina folded the girl into her arms. Dolores had not cried in hours, but she began crying now. Chacho stared at her, wondering if women cried only when they had a willing audience. He decided he was being unduly harsh; grief was a thing to be shared, and now she had someone else with whom she must share it.

Benito looked up at Chacho, who still sat on the sorrel mare. "Will you not get down, Chacho? There is food in the house."

Chacho shook his head. "There are still some miles to be made before it is dark."

Benito read a lot into the harried expression on Chacho's face. "Someone is after you."

Chacho nodded gravely. "I tried to throw them off the trail a long way back. Sometimes these gringos are easily fooled. But if there is a wise one among them, they may still be after me. It would be well that I move on."

Old Benito was puzzled. "Mexico is to the south. Where are you going that you ride north?"

Chacho shook his head. "They cannot force you to tell something that you do not know. It is better for you as well as me that you know as little as possible."

The old farmer accepted that. "You should take a little to eat, at least. And there is coffee in the house. A little coffee will give you strength. Go, eat and drink a little while I water your mare for you. She needs drink, even if you do not."

That kind of logic reached Chacho where little else would. He eased himself to the ground, swaying a little from fatigue. "You are a kind man, *Tio*."

"I always sympathize with the horse." He started to lead the mare to the trough but held back, his brow deeply furrowed. "Would you want to tell me what bad thing has happened?"

Chacho shoved his hands into his pockets and looked away. "I have killed a gringo *cherife*."

The old man automatically crossed himself, whispering something Chacho could not hear . . . a prayer of some kind. At length *Tio* Benito said, "It is madness for you to go north, then. They will hunt you down like the wolf that has killed the sheep. Go south, *hijo*, to Mexico."

"Everybody runs south to Mexico. That is where they will look for me. I will go where no one would expect to find me."

"They will find you. They always find whoever they look for, these *rinches*, these *cherifes*. There is no safe place except Mexico."

The old man meant well, Chacho realized that. He reminded him gently, "You were going to water my mare."

Chacho ate some roast goat and a cold flour tortilla, sipping at a cup of steaming black coffee while he listened to Dolores tearfully telling her aunt what had happened . . . her own version, based on what she had seen. The old people would come out of this blaming Chacho, at least in part, and he regretted it. But that was one of his smaller concerns at the moment.

He could have eaten more, but he saw Benito leading the mare back from water. Chacho picked up one more flour tortilla to carry with him, putting a little of the goat meat in it and rolling it up. "*Tia* . . . Dolores . . . adiós."

The old woman seemed torn between blame and sympathy. "Be careful."

Dolores stared, not answering him. But as he walked out under the vine-covered arbor that served the purpose of a porch, she came to the door and called in a broken voice, "Chacho." She stood in the opening, tears shining on her full cheeks. She said, "What is done is done. Go with God."

He spurred out of the farmhouse yard and up the narrow trail that led northward.

Finding the unpainted frame house of Baudelio Aguilar in the darkness would be no great problem for Chacho. He had found it in the night many times before, for he had worked as long as there was light, then had gone courting Luisa.

Now that he approached the place he began having misgivings. He had never stood in the good graces of the old señora; she had opposed him from the start, certain that if her daughter would cast her smiles in another direction she could come up with a far better catch. To be sure, old Baudelio had looked upon Chacho with favor, and that should have been all he needed. It was popularly supposed that in Mexican families the man ruled absolutely, but anybody who totally believed that was likely to be mistaken about other things as well. The old lady would probably raise all kinds of hell when she heard the trouble Chacho was in. It would prove that everything she had been saying was true. It would be like her to get word to the *rinches* if she thought that would save her daughter from becoming forever tied to a man of Chacho's lowly estate.

Damn an old woman like that, he thought darkly, wondering how Baudelio had ever let himself into such a trap. But, of course, if he hadn't there would have been no Luisa. A man had to suffer, sometimes, to attain the prize.

He began to wonder if it might not be wise to talk to Baudelio first, to bolster the old man's faith in him before it underwent the inevitable assault from the old lady. To ride down to the farm now would be to wade deep into a violent argument. Perhaps it would be better to send an emissary, someone who could bring Baudelio to him and give Chacho time to tell his own story in his own way.

He thought then of the Bustamante family. He had worked in the cottonfields with Diego Bustamante and had gained the everlasting gratitude and friendship of the aged grandfather Esteban by listening with interest to his wild yarns of revolution in Mexico. It was Esteban who had, for a time, gotten Chacho involved in running horses to the border.

The Bustamantes would appreciate the hell he had been through and would intercede for him with Baudelio. He knew for a fact that Baudelio put great stock in patriarch Esteban's judgment on almost anything. After all, did Esteban not carry the scars of bayonet and rifle ball? Had he not fought against Maximilian's *imperialistas* on the Mexico side of the Rio Grande, and against the gringos in the border wars with the wily Juan Cortina? That had been in his youth some forty years ago, and his old bones were brittle now, but his mind was as sharp and clear as it had ever been. He was a man people listened to.

Chacho thought he knew how to find the Bustamante place, but in the dark he became confused and had to give up. He could feel the mare failing beneath him and knew he had pushed her harder than a man had a right to do. He dismounted, staked the mare at the end of his rope to give her good grazing room, then spread the single blanket he had tied behind his saddle. Only when he stretched himself out full length did he fully realize how tired he was. Every muscle in his body seemed to ache. He knew it was a good thing he had eaten what he did at the house of Tio Benito, for this was a dry camp and would have been a hungry one. He had brought no food from home.

He needed sleep, but sleep was a long time in coming. Lying here in the still night, listening to the rustle of small night-prowling hunters and to the night-singing birds in the mesquites, he kept reliving the day's tragedy until cold sweat seemed to soak his thin cotton clothing and leave him shivering in the warmth of June. A hundred times he saw the sheriff's face in the moment of death, until at last he cried out to the gringo *cherife* to go away and for the sake of God to let him alone. "I did not want to shoot you," Chacho cried. "I would give up my own life . . . to see you alive again."

Sleep came, finally, a fitful sleep harried by awesome dreams . . . of *rinches* by the hundreds, of sheriffs and angry gringo faces crying for the blood of Chacho Fernandez. All night he seemed to be running, so that when he awoke to find the sunrise hurting his eyes, he was still tired.

He did not want to get up. His body ached for more rest. But awakening brought a rush of recollections. For a moment he was almost in panic, his sleep-drugged mind running riot with all manner of terrible suppositions. But gradually as he sorted things into their proper places he came back to a calm of sorts, to a perspective in which self-preservation became the major and almost only priority.

He began to think in probabilities. It was probable that most if not all of the hunt was going on to the south, that he was already beyond the most pressing danger. True, there was always a possibility that some sharp-eyed gringo might stumble across the tracks he and Dolores had made after they had finally left the creek, but this had to be considered unlikely. Even if it did happen, a man following tracks seldom could move as rapidly as the man who made them. Darkness would have stopped him in any case. Even at worst, Chacho figured he had some time. If lucky, he was already in the clear.

His stomach was angry with him, and he wished he had taken time to bring some food. The sorrel mare was cropping at the grass; at least she would not be hungry. And surely she had rested more than Chacho, for she had no bad dreams to haunt her. It would not be far to the Bustamantes', and then a little back this way to Baudelio Aguilar's. Saddling, he looked at the sign he was leaving. Anybody who followed the trail this far would know at a glance that he had spent the night here. The mare had grazed considerably within the circle allowed her by the stake rope, and she had left droppings.

Well, anybody who gets this far will be hard to fool anyway, he thought. As he saw it now, his safety lay not in getting away from people but in getting among them, where his own trail would become lost amid those of others, and where his individual identity would become lost amid thousands of other Mexican people.

He was not altogether sure of his bearings, but he was confident that after he had ridden awhile and full daylight came, he would pick up some familiar landmark. It would be hard to get him permanently lost in this part of the country in daytime; he had been over most of it.

As he expected, he soon came across a familiar trail. He had long since learned the frontiersman's way of pausing every so often to look behind him on a new trail so he would know how it appeared when he came back facing the other direction. One aspect was sometimes vastly different from another.

Soon he spotted a windmill a mile ahead, its huge cypress fan standing high above the mesquite and chaparral. Something about it sparked a memory. He was sure he had ridden up to this one late on a summer afternoon and had run head-on into a swarm of wasps. He had spurred away, scratching at several fast-rising welts. He had come back at dusk, when the wasps went in. He had kindled a fire and burned the nest away. A thing like that, a man did not forget.

He saw no fresh horse tracks in the trail; nobody had been here since sometime yesterday. He did not want to leave any of his own that might be questioned by some casual passerby, so he rode off to one side, paralleling, holding the mare as much as possible to the grassy ground where her tracks would be difficult to see.

He was sure of the windmill. He approached it carefully, knowing that travelers often camped by the mills at night to have access to the water. It made him wonder, sometimes, how the old ones ever got along in the water-shy country before they learned how to drill wells and put up windmills. The thought made him glad he was living in this modern time rather than in the primitive days of his grandfathers. He had heard it said that a man could get on the railroad cars at one end of the nation and reach the other in just a few days, sleeping on sheets in a fine bed. He could not imagine why anyone would want to travel so far, but it was a wondrous thing that they could do it if they wanted to.

He looked up at a great gray hawk, slowly circling, seeking its morning breakfast. *Well, old bird,* he thought, *no man will ever crowd you up there where you are. One thing man will never do is fly.* Right now he wished he could.

Chacho found no campers at the mill, just a handful of cattle that had spent the night bedded down nearby. Most cattle trailed in to water during the hot afternoons, drank their fill, rested awhile, then drank again and scattered back out on the grass before night came. But among cattle as among people there were always some that never chose to range far from water. Chacho rode in slowly so as not to run them off. If he could get by without unduly disturbing them, there was a good chance they would come up to water after he was gone, and their stirring would cover his tracks.

He loosened the girth to let the mare drink all she wanted. At this time of day, neither hot nor tired yet, there was little risk she would overdo it. Chacho bellied down next to the pipe that fed the water out from the mill into the big open surface tank. He cupped his hands and drank fresh water at the mouth of the pipe. He had known times he was thirsty enough to drink with the cattle and horses, but there had not been many. That was for a savage, not for a civilized man.

The windmill had given him his direction. The Bustamante place was five — maybe six — miles north and a little to the west. Over that way the land flattened a little, and much of it had been broken out for cotton and feed grains in the last ten or fifteen years. Cattle always gave way wherever a crop could be grown that produced more money and let more people find a place on the land.

Chacho had not gone a mile past the mill when he discovered movement ahead. Tensing, he pulled the mare into the cover of a nearby thicket of mesquite and mixed brush, staying near enough to the edge that he could keep his eyes on whatever it was that he had seen.

Directly he made out that they were horsemen, perhaps half a dozen of them, coming down the trail in his direction. *Vaqueros,* he hoped, out gathering cattle for their *patrón.* But in time he could tell they were not Mexican, they were *Americanos,* all riding good stout horses, every man carrying a rifle and wearing a pistol on his hip. Chacho eased to the ground and covered the mare's nose with his hand, just in case she might have a tendency toward sociability. He watched dry-mouthed as they rode within fifty yards of him.

He was thankful he had taken the precaution of not using the trail. He looked back at the windmill, worrying. If the cattle had not come to water, and if these men were watchful, they would see his tracks.

Perhaps they would not notice. Why should they be watching for tracks this far to the north? He had put a lot of miles behind him. Surely no one up here knew what had happened at the Frisco place.

He waited until the men were well gone before he swung back into the saddle. His shirt was half soaked with sweat. That surprised him; the morning was not yet hot.

Get control of yourself, Chacho, or you will be jumping from every jackrabbit you see.

At one point he was within sight of Baudelio Aguilar's place and the temptation was strong to ride down there. But he had thought this out yesterday. He knew he had better see the Bustamantes first.

He had to cross the trail eventually to get there. He broke a small branch from a mesquite and walked back to brush out the mare's tracks. He carried the branch awhile and dropped it inconspicuously beside another mesquite. As he rode, he kept looking over his shoulder for sign the gringos were coming back. He told himself he had misjudged them, that they were simply cowboys, perhaps on their way south to pick up a herd. But he kept thinking about all those guns. Well, maybe they were carrying money to buy cattle, and they needed the guns to protect themselves.

That was a lie, and he knew it. Somehow he realized his first instincts had been right. They were lawmen. At the least, they were deputized civilians. They weren't hunting for cattle. Deep down he knew: *they are hunting for me.*

A cold feeling built in the pit of his stomach and stayed there. He made his approach to the Bustamante farm from the brushiest side and stopped in the edge of the chaparral to study the place. For a full twenty minutes he stayed there, not sure what he was looking for. With some misgivings he finally ventured out. He was halfway across the clearing when Diego Bustamante waved at him from a field of young corn, dropped his hoe and came trotting to meet him.

Diego was half out of breath. "Chacho!" he exclaimed, as if not quite believing. "Is it really you?"

"I am not a ghost." Chacho was bewildered at the strangeness in Diego's face. "At least not yet."

Diego looked apprehensively in all directions. "What are you doing, riding in broad daylight this way?"

Chacho realized that Diego knew. But how could he, so far north? "Why shouldn't I?"

"Do you not know that every officer from here to the Rio Grande is out today looking for you? This minute there may be a hundred of them a mile behind you."

Involuntarily Chacho turned to look.

Diego pointed to the house. "We will hide the mare in the shed. You are probably hungry and thirsty. We have a little *pulque* in the house; it will pick you up. You are sure there is not a bunch of officers just behind you?"

"I figured all the *rinches* would be chasing shadows to the south."

"There are *rinches* enough these days anywhere a man goes. They grow up like weeds in the new corn."

In a few minutes they had the mare hidden behind the tall stone fence of a small corral which opened into a squatty shed built of mesquite trunks and limbs stacked between upright posts and covered over with brush and sod. The Bustamante family was poor, like almost everyone in this country, but there was always a little corn for the horses. Diego Bustamante dipped a tin bucket into a wooden barrel and poured corn into a trough hollowed out of a huge old mesquite trunk.

Diego stared at the sorrel. "It is said you killed a sheriff over a stolen mare."

"This is the one. But she was not stolen, except from me. They tried to steal her from me."

"I thought as much. These lawmen, they always lie." He turned his attention back to Chacho. "You are surely hungry."

As they approached the dwelling — a cheaply built gringo frame much like the one on the Frisco place — Chacho could see old Esteban Bustamante sitting outside on the little porch. It was not like the old man to be sitting around at this time of day; he had always been a worker.

"Your father is sick?" he asked Diego.

"A little. And he was upset over the news about you. He thinks highly of you, Chacho. He fears they will kill you."

Old Esteban's brown eyes blinked in disbelief, then brimmed with joyful tears as be became sure. "Chacho! It is really you. I thought by now they had surely found and shot you."

"It is me, Grandfather. I am all right. They will not find me."

"Thanks to God." The old man pushed up from his chair to embrace Chacho in the way of the olden times. Chacho made a sign for Esteban to seat himself again, to take his ease. Chacho's hat was in his hand, a sign of respect. He would never consider speaking to this old man with his hat on. "It is good to see you, Grandfather. But it is not good to see you sitting in the shade at this time of the day. I do not like to find you ill."

"I feel better already, seeing your face, *mi hijo*. It is better for me than a drink of *pulque*." He looked around impatiently. "Where is the *pulque*? Are there no women in the house? Can you not see that we have a guest? Bring us the *pulque*."

They brought it out in a goatskin bag, Diego's wife and his pretty young daughter Juanita. They gave it to Chacho, but he deferred until Esteban had taken a long swallow or two, then turned it up. It burned all the way to his toes; it was fine. He wiped his dusty sleeve across his mouth and handed the bag to Diego.

When Diego was through, Esteban began demanding that the women bring Chacho something to eat. They rushed to his bidding. He might have been old, and he might have lost the speed and dash of his youth, but he had lost none of his forcefulness.

Esteban's eyes bored into Chacho, speculating. "Is it true, *hijo*? Did you really kill the gringo *cherife*?"

Chacho lowered his eyes. "Yes, Grandfather, it is true."

To his surprise the old man laughed aloud and slapped the palm of his hand against his bony knee. "*Ay*, what I would have given to have seen it!"

71

Chacho said, "It was not a proud thing."

"But of course it was a proud thing. Do you know that in all my life and in all the battles I fought when I was a young man, I never killed a genuine *cherife*? A few gringo soldiers and once a deputy of some kind, but never a *cherife*."

"I did not want to kill him. It was all a misunderstanding.

"Do not make light of it. When a man has done a big thing, he has a right to feel proud. Our people will honor you, for this, Chacho."

The unanswered question came back. "But how do they know? How do you know? It happened only yesterday, and a long way from here."

Diego put in, "It is the gringo telephone. Do you not know how they can talk through the wires? They have given the news all the way to the capital in Austin, to the headquarters of all the *rinches*. It has come to every county *cherife* in this part of Texas. Our people in town, they heard of it, yesterday after it came over the telephone. We knew of it last night."

Last night! Chacho groaned, remembering how secure he had felt last night over the distance he had traveled.

Diego said, "From all to the north of here, officers are coming south to join in the hunt. We have seen some already today, passing by, looking us over and riding on. It is a wonder you have missed them."

"I almost ran into some," Chacho said, shivering a little as full realization of his dilemma came home to him. Perhaps the north was nowhere nearly so safe as he had envisioned.

"I have known of the telephone," he said, "but somehow I did not fully understand how far it could reach. I did not realize that news could travel faster than a horse could run."

Old Esteban snorted. "The telephone! Another gringo trick. You can never make those people fight fair."

To the gray-bearded patriarch this was another battle in the old racial wars. It was a simple matter of good against evil, and anything gringo was evil.

It was this philosophy that Esteban had used on Chacho to get him involved for a while in the running of stolen horses. To Esteban they were not stolen if they were taken from a gringo; they were *recovered*, as the land would someday be recovered. They were the spoils of an unfinished war that would continue as long as he and the others like him on either side still lived. He could rationalize his activity as patriotism. For a time he had convinced Chacho.

Chacho said, "The sheriff was not a bad man. He was misled by a bad man. I wish I could have killed the bad man and let the sheriff live."

"They are all bad," the old man argued, his bony finger pointed at Chacho. "When you are my age you will know. We should have killed them all; there was a time we could have, if we could have gotten all our people to agree. One day we will yet kill them all."

Chacho realized the futility of arguing with Esteban and nodded agreement in the hope that would end the discussion. A man of Esteban's age had the old hatreds burned so deeply on his soul that he could never be expected to change. Chacho said to Esteban and Diego, "I came here hoping you could help me."

"Hide you?" Diego said. "Certainly we will do that."

"That too, but there is something else. I hoped you could go with me to see Baudelio and Luisa. I want to explain this thing to them. It would help if I had the two of you to back me up. If I am lucky I can go on north and find a place of safety. I can send for Luisa."

The old man shook his head, and Chacho saw disapproval in Diego's eyes. He added quickly, "I would not send for her until it was completely safe. I would not have her take any risk."

Diego said, "It is not that, it is the risk today that I am concerned about. You cannot ride over to Baudelio's. There is too much chance you would run into officers."

"But I've got to talk to them."

The old man said, "Let it go, *hijo*. There are women

73

wherever a man may go. You do not need this Luisa. There will be many others as pretty."

"I do not want any others. I want her."

"But the risk. . . . A man can cut all his ties, but a woman never will. Sbe would write to her people, or come to visit them. The *rinches* would be on you like wolves. Six months, a year, five years . . . a *rinche* never forgets."

Chacho did not want to argue with the old man, but on this point he could not yield. "I will not leave until I see her."

Diego gazed across the cornfield, his brow creased in worry. He shrugged regretfully. "I will go and bring them here."

The old man kept up his protest, but the thing was done. His voice trailed off angrily in mid-sentence as he gave it up . . . almost. When Diego had gone to the shed, Esteban resumed his argument. "I tell you, Chacho, when you are my age and the hot blood has cooled, you will see that one woman is about like another. If she can sew and cook . . . and is cooperative in her attitude . . . that is all a man needs of her. The prettiest of them grow fat or get lines in their faces like the furrows in a field, and then one cannot remember which was pretty and which was homely."

Chacho had not smiled in a long time, but he smiled now. "Grandfather, my blood is still hot, and I can see the dfference. Why should I stare at a homely woman all these years, waiting until I become old enough that it no longer matters?"

The old man saw nothing funny. He glared. "You will never get that old if you do not listen to good advice. . . ."

Chacho felt obliged to explain to Esteban how the trouble had arisen in the first place, that it had all come about because of the sorrel mare he wanted to earn as a gift for Luisa. He told it all, the trader's betrayal, the sheriff's visit, the shooting.

"As you can see," he summed up, "the wrong people died . . . my brother, the sheriff. I should have killed that Barnhill when he first tried to cheat me."

"He was a gringo. To cheat is in their nature, as it is in the nature of a cat to chase the birds. The sheriff would have come after you in any case. In any case you would have had to kill him. It was all planned, Chacho, up there." He looked up toward Heaven. "It was all foreordained by the God who looks out for our people. You have become His instrument of vengeance, don't you see?"

Chacho shook his head. "God would not work this way. He would not work through a crooked horse-dealer and an interpreter who does not know the language."

"He works in mysterious ways, have the priests not said so again and again? He sends the wolf so the rabbits do not overpopulate the earth. Perhaps He has sent you to deliver us from the gringo."

It was fortunate that the women called Chacho into the house to eat, for he was on the verge of arguing with the old man, a thing he had no wish to do. He revered old Esteban, even if he could no longer agree with him.

He ate eagerly and drank a considerable amount of coffee. He noticed that the two women sat across the small kitchen and stared at him in a strange way — not frightened, but somehow awed by what he had done. They had known him a long time and had always treated him as one of the family. Had it not been for Luisa, he probably would have given Diego's pretty daughter a try, to see what nature might lead to. He had always thought she would be willing. But she looked at him now as if he were some stranger.

When Chacho had eaten his fill, Diego's wife said, "You look tired. You did not sleep much last night."

Chacho shook his head. He supposed it showed.

The woman said, "Take a nap, then. You can use Esteban's bed."

The thought was appealing. "What if officers come?"

"We will keep watch," she promised. "All of us."

Esteban had a small room, really nothing more than a lean-to, which he shared with Diego's fifteen-year-old son Anselmo. His bed was not much, a goatskin spread over a cornhusk mattress on top of a wooden frame, a moth-eaten old blanket folded at the foot so that he might cover himself against the night's chill. These old ones, these veterans of the long trails, seldom let themselves become slaves to creature comfort.

Chacho started to take off his boots but thought better of it. He would hate to have to run barefoot. He stretched out on the goatskin, the cornhusks uncomfortably lumpy beneath him. He was tempted to move the skin to the floor. It would be hard, but at least it would be even. He looked up and saw Diego's daughter Juanita staring at him through the open door.

Damn, but she was turning into a handsome woman.

The girl said, "Do you want me to shut the door, Chacho?"

He nodded. She shut it, from the inside. He looked at her a moment, wishing. Then he shook his head. "From the outside, Juanita. "

Even if he had wanted to keep her here, old Esteban and her mother were too near. His thoughts went then to Luisa. He was ashamed for relishing a momentary temptation.

SEVEN

This place gave him a feeling of security. That and his full belly helped him drop off to sleep. He had no idea how long he had been lying there when Diego's wife gently shook him. "Diego is coming back. Someone is following him in a wagon."

Chacho raised up, yawning, and thanked her. He stood cautiously a moment in the open front door, though he knew there was little reason for uneasiness. Old Esteban sat on the porch, a rifle across his lap. If anything untoward had happened, the old man would have fired first and investigated later.

Diego's face was unaccountably grim as he dismounted. "I brought them," he said. His voice was clipped, almost bitter. Chacho stepped out hurriedly to greet Luisa Aguilar and her father, Baudelio. He raised his hands to help her step down. To his surprise, she seemed to shrink back from him.

Baudelio stared, his eyes not friendly. "I suspected it

might be you. Diego would not tell us why he wanted us to come; he just insisted that we do it. I suspected it was for you."

Chacho was taken aback. He knew now that they had heard of his trouble; he had hoped he could tell them first himself. He raised his hands again for Luisa. Baudelio caught her arm and motioned for her to stay on the springless seat. He said, "We heard about you, Chacho. We thought you would run for Mexico."

Baudelio's coldness was like a slap across Chacho's face, painful and unexpected. He explained that he knew the law would be more watchful to the south than to the north.

Chacho looked at Luisa. "I had to see you, to ask you to wait for me. When I am safe and settled, I will send for you."

Baudelio glared. "You may send all you want to, Chacho, but she will not go."

Chacho's jaw sagged. "Baudelio. . . ."

The girl's father said, "Every officer in Texas will be looking for you. If they don't get you today, they'll get you tomorrow. If they don't get you tomorrow they'll get you next week, or next month, or next year. You want to drag my daughter along with you while you run? No, Chacho. You got into this trouble by yourself. You will not drag my daughter into it with you."

Chacho turned to Luisa. "I wanted no trouble. This all happened because I wanted to buy a pretty mare for you to ride. I earned her. It was all fair and honest, and then they tried to steal her. They tried to steal your mare, Luisa."

He saw tears in her eyes, but she made no move to get down.

Anxiously he said, "I have the mare out in the shed. She is the most beautiful thing you ever saw." He trotted toward the shed, looking back to be sure the wagon did not move. He slipped a bridle over the sorrel mare's head and led her out of the pen, trotting. She trotted along behind him, never letting the reins lose their slack.

"She is yours, Luisa. No matter what they say, I earned her. I give her to you. Take her."

Luisa never budged. Whatever tears had welled up, she had blinked away. Chacho saw a hardness in her eyes now much like the hardness in the eyes of Baudelio. "For that, you killed a man? Better you had shot the mare than the man."

"I wanted her for you."

"She has blood on her; I don't want her. You have blood on you, too. Get away from here before you bring trouble on all of us."

"Luisa. . . ."

"Go, Chacho!"

Baudelio said, "You should never have come here. You should have gone to Mexico. Do not ever come to us again. If you ever try to see Luisa, I will go to the *rinches* myself. Do you understand me, Chacho?"

Chacho slumped. He stared in disbelief at the revulsion in Luisa's face. Baudelio said, "You listen to what I tell you, Chacho. Stay away. Never come back here or you are dead!" Baudelio flipped the reins and set the team of brown Mexican mules to moving. He turned them and started back up the same winding road on which he had come.

Diego muttered bitterly, "They will betray you, Chacho. I feel it in my gut; they will betray you."

Old Esteban nodded. "They would, but they will never get the chance." He raised the rifle to his shoulder.

Chacho found his voice. He shouted "No!" and shoved the muzzle downward. The old man tried to wrestle it from his hand, but Chacho had a strong grip. "You are a fool, Chacho!"

"Too many people have already died." He turned, still holding the rifle, forcing the muzzle toward the ground. He stared after the departing wagon, its passengers blissfully unaware how near they had come to death. They seemed to blur out. "I still love her, Esteban."

The old man gave up with a shrug. "I say it again. You are a fool."

It was decided that Chacho should remain until dark. There was always a chance Baudelio would hunt up an officer and give him away, but they agreed it was unlikely. Should an officer approach Baudelio and ask him, Baudelio probably would not hesitate to tell.

Diego said, "One has to weigh the risks, one against the other. The risk that you would run into officers out there in the daylight is probably greater than the risk of your being found here before dark."

The boy Anselmo came in at noon from his work with the cattle and saw Chacho for the first time. He was eager to know all the details, and his eyes seemed to glow as he heard his father recount them; Chacho did not feel like talking. The boy seemed especially pleased about the sheriff. He had been listening too much to his grandfather.

That damned old man will get himself killed someday, and everybody around him, Chacho thought.

Anselmo said, "Chacho, four eyes can watch better than two. Let me go with you. I will help you watch out for the *rinches.*"

Chacho saw alarm leap into the eyes of the boy's mother and father, although he saw pride in Esteban's. The old man would heartily approve. Chacho shook his head. "Two horses leave twice as many tracks. You stay here, boy. Your parents need you."

Anselmo argued a little, but under no circumstances would Chacho accept him, and the boy soon saw that. When the family had finished the noon meal, they scattered to their individual chores. Esteban went back to his vigil on the front porch, the rifle across his lap. Anselmo rode back out to the cattle. Diego and his wife walked into the cornfield, hoes in their hands. The girl stayed near the house, hoeing in a garden.

Chacho tried to sleep again, knowing he would probably ride all night. But it was not in him any more. He got up, stepped out onto the porch and stood a few silent moments with Esteban, then walked on to the shed. He went into the pen and looked at the mare. He found a brush and caught her and began to brush her down, talking to her all the while, telling her they had a long hard trip ahead of them.

He became aware that he was not alone. He spun, his breath stopping short. The pistol seemed to leap into his hand.

He saw the girl Juanita, standing in the partially opened gate. She was momentarily frightened by the pistol but eased after he put it back into his waistband. She closed the gate behind her and walked up slowly. She said, "She is a very pretty mare." But her eyes were not on the mare; they were on Chacho.

He was still struggling for breath after the scare. "Yes, she is."

"I wish someone had thought enough of me to want to give me a mare like this one."

"You are young. There will be a lot of men, I'll bet."

"There has always been only one that I ever really wanted."

He sensed the direction her talk was leading. "Don't you think you had better go back to the house?"

"I am not in the house. I am hoeing the garden."

"Not right now, you are not."

"She never was the girl for you, Chacho. She had a pretty face, I will agree with that, but she was always a weak woman beneath, and a little silly."

"I do not want to talk about it .

"Neither do I, but it needed saying. When you think about it, you will know I am right." She moved closer, close enough to bring her within touching distance. She placed her hand on his arm. "I am not a weak woman. And I hope I am not being silly."

"You are being foolish."

"I do not think so." She had both arms around him, and her face was upturned. She raised up on tiptoe and kissed him, her hands pressing against his back to bring him down to her a little. He tried to resist the warmth that started rising in his blood. But when she brought the full length of her body against him he was lost. She kissed him again, and this time he brought his arms up around her, letting the fire run wild.

She said, "When you ride away from here you are going to be thinking of *me*, Chacho, and not of that silly Luisa."

She turned a little, not letting go of him, and led him into the coolness of the dark shed.

At dusk Chacho saddled the mare. Diego and Esteban were beside him in the pen, and Anselmo stood sorrowfully at the gate, wishing he could go. Diego said, "We are agreed then? Since you told Baudelio that you planned to go north, and since it is likely that he will tell this to the first officer who asks him, it is better that you do now what you should have done in the beginning. Try to get to Mexico."

Chacho nodded regretfully. It had been a bitter decision. "It will be much harder now. They will be going over that country like a rake over a yard."

Esteban squatted despite the pain in his arthritic knees. He sketched a rude map in the sand with his bony finger. "But you have some advantage, *hijo*. You have been up and down the line with horses, dodging gringo officers. You know where the secret stopping places are. You know where you can get food, and where there is water. You know where you can find our people to help you."

Diego shook his head vigorously. "That was a different thing, papa. There it was only horses. This time he has killed an officer. By now it is likely that the gringos have offered a big reward for him. There are those even among our own people who would turn him in if the reward is large enough."

Esteban stared incredulously at his son. "Our own people? That is impossible."

"Have we not already agreed that Baudelio will tell? There are many who are hungry, papa. Offer them enough money . . . Jesus Christ himself was betrayed for thirty pieces of silver. Chacho is not Jesus." Diego looked Chacho in the eyes. "It is better you are seen by no one, not our people or anyone else. Use the trails but stay away from people. You cannot know now which ones are still your friends."

Esteban was shaking his gray head, unable to cope with the idea of treason. He punched a hole in the sand near the bottom of his map. "There is one I would trust with my life. That is Julio Carrasco. You know where he lives, Chacho, near the river. You have turned horses over to him, and he has taken them across." Esteban drew a wiggly line that represented the river and punched again the spot near-by that represented the home of Julio Carrasco. "Carrasco knows all the places. He will know how to take you to the river and get you across under the noses of a thousand *rinches*. Whatever else you do, go to Carrasco. Tell him I sent you. By yourself you might be caught. With Carrasco to help you there are not gringos enough in all Texas to find you."

Chacho looked to Diego, not sure he could trust the old man's faith. Diego nodded affirmation. "In Carrasco's case, I think it is safe. If you can reach Carrasco you will be all right. The problem will be to get that far."

Julio Carrasco was a fanatic of old Esteban's stripe, one who would fight until they buried him. Then they would have to place a heavy stone slab over his grave or he would dig out.

Chacho checked the goatskin bags he had tied behind the cantle of his saddle; they held food the women had prepared for his journey. He looked to the west and no longer saw any sign of color in the sky. "It is time," he said somberly. He cast a glance at the women, coming out from the house to see him off. He shook hands with Diego and Esteban and Anselmo. He spoke to Diego's wife and held out one hand to Juanita.

Juanita's fingers pressed hard against his own. He knew she wanted to kiss him but would not, not in front of the others. Very softly she said, "If you ever sent for me, Chacho, I would go."

He had no answer to give her. If he reached Mexico there would be time then to analyze his feelings, to see if they were truly deep or if he had simply responded to a transient need. "If I get there, I will find a way to let you know . . . all of you."

"Go with God, Chacho," Juanita cried.

He knew there was no practical way here to cover his tracks. There was too much sand. He cut straight for the brush which would hide him, then headed south as directly as he could figure it. Later, when the stars came out, he knew one which led to the river. He would ride all night, not worrying about finding a familiar trail. At daylight he could probably find some landmark and get himself oriented. The main thing now was to travel as far and as fast as he could.

He was perhaps two miles from the Bustamante place when he heard a sudden burst of gunfire behind him. It was rapid, more shots than he could count. He hauled the mare up suddenly, turning her around with a jerk on the bits that was harder than he intended.

His blood went cold. *Good God, they're killing them all!*

He touched spurs to the mare and put her into a hard run, straight back toward the sound of the shooting.

But in a short time, the space of two or three minutes, the shooting stopped. He pulled up, gentler this time, and stood in the stirrups, listening. It was over. Whatever had happened, it was over and done with.

A rush of helpless rage set him to cursing aloud. He touched spurs to the mare and began running again, pistol in his hand. Whatever they had done, those *rinches*, he would make them pay!

But gradually reason took control of him. There was nothing he could do for the family now. It would be of no help to them if he rode in there and got himself killed. He stopped and shoved the pistol back into his waistband. The faces all came to him in a crushing moment of guilt ...

Diego and his wife, Anselmo, Esteban ... Juanita. Were they all dead, or dying? Had they been taken prisoner? There was no way to know now except to go back, and to go back meant certain capture or death. Then the Bustamantes' sacrifice would have been for nothing.

He could not go back . . . he could not throw all that away.

He cried out in anguish and called upon God to show him what to do. But God gave him no answer. Chacho looked to the dark skies but saw only the stars, beginning to come out.

He knew what he had to do, hard as it was. He turned his back on the Bustamantes and set the mare into a trot again, heading south. By the stars.

EIGHT

Sancho Creek stopped Kelly Sadler and Joe Florey. It was easy enough to find where the two horses had crossed over. Then suddenly the tracks were lost amid those of many horses. Kelly could see a scattering of loose horses and a couple of mules grazing near the creek bottom.

Florey had not said a half dozen words after setting out on the trail of Chacho Fernandez. He said nothing now beyond a little frustrated cursing, half under his breath as he circled the Frisco horses and tried to pick up some meaningful sign.

Kelly rode close to him, watching the creek bank and the chaparral closely. This would be a good place, he thought, for somebody to set up an ambush. He carried his rifle across the pommel, his right hand across the trigger guard. But there was no ambush. There was only the frustration of a trail suddenly lost amid the confusion of many tracks.

Joe Florey reined up finally, shaking his head. "That's one damn smart Mexican."

Kelly looked back in the direction from where they had come. "I see Willcox and the others, ridin' up. If we don't stop them they'll come chargin' in here and we never will find the right tracks."

"Go stop them, then. I'll keep lookin' around."

Kelly was dubious about leaving Florey without protection, but Florey impatiently waved him off. "Go on, dammit!"

Kelly caught the posse as it was crossing the creek, and he got the men stopped. He explained about the lost trail and the need to stay back. The men were faunching at the bits and ready to go on, but Kelly was firm about it. For a minute he thought he might have to climb down and whip somebody. Deputy Odom Willcox finally shrugged and looked back over his shoulder.

"Everybody get down and let your horses blow a little. We'll give the old man time to hunt. If he don't come up with somethin' pretty quick we'll go and help him."

Florey found nothing. Soon the possemen were scattered for half a mile in all directions, but mostly south, riding back and forth looking for a sign. Some probably knew what to look for; others were simply making a mess of any sign that might have existed.

Willcox finally rode to catch up with Joe Florey, who was trying to stay south of them all, Kelly still siding him. Willcox began shouting and waving his hat when he was still a hundred yards away. Florey squinted, knowing Willcox by the horse he rode and by the way he sat in the saddle. "Wisht you'd look at him," he grumbled, long before Willcox reached him. "Hollerin' like that. . . . He couldn't slip up on a deaf-and-dumb Kansas City drummer, three days dead. Hell, in the old days we wouldn't've let him wash out the spittoons in company headquarters."

"Guess they're not raisin' peace officers like they used to," Kelly said, making it a point to agree with Joe.

"They sure ain't. The blood has thinned out."

Willcox made a fuss about the time they were wasting trying to pick up a trail when everybody knew the Mexican was running as hard as he could for Mexico. Just head south, Willcox argued, and they couldn't miss. Sooner or later they were bound to cut the trail again. It would be a lot fresher than any they might finally find here.

Florey plainly wanted to curse, but he was holding himself back. He looked at Kelly. Kelly had nothing to say; frankly, he thought Willcox was probably right.

To Kelly's surprise, Joe Florey gradually began to seem relieved. "Well now, Odom, you and your boys just go right on. If you want to move, I don't see why you ought to let a slow old man like me hold you back."

Odom was caught off guard, too, and he seemed suddenly suspicious. "You tryin' to get rid of us, Joe?"

"Just tryin' to help. You want to go runnin' off after that Mexican, you go right ahead. I'll just keep on lookin' for tracks. If you're right, fine; you'll likely catch him. If you're wrong, at least you won't be spoilin' the trail for me. You-all go on."

Odom seemed a little less sure of himself, but he said, "That's what we'll do, Joe." As he pulled his horse away he kept looking at Joe, wondering.

Florey dismissed him by turning his back. He studied Kelly with a critical eye. "How about you? Why don't you go with him? I know you agree with him."

"I promised I'd side you."

"I didn't ask you to make that promise; I won't hold you to it."

"I'll stay with you." He said it stubbornly, and Joe Florey had good qualifications to recognize stubborness. Joe accepted with a nod. He sat his horse awhile, watching Odom gather up his posse and start moving south with it in a long trot. It was plain that he felt better. As a tracker he had always worked best when he didn't have a lot of people pressing on him, especially people in whom he had little confidence. These men weren't peace officers, most of them. They were cowboys and merchants and God knew what else, good men in their own fields but out of place in a situation like this.

Florey frowned as he watched the men disappear in the

late-afternoon sun. "They're in worse danger from each other than from that Mexican."

Joe worked back gradually to the creek and sat looking down into it. "I got a strong feelin' about this creek," he said. "I think he rode out into them horses to lose his tracks, then got back into the creek to cover his trail. Question is, did he go down the creek or up it?"

"Down. That's the way to Mexico."

"That's what everybody says. It's what any man would be apt to do under the circumstances. But did he? We've already found out he's smart."

Kelly saw what Joe was driving at, but he couldn't accept it. "You sayin' he went north? The only safety for him is south."

"Maybe. But there's lots of Mexicans to the north of here. One more wouldn't be noticed. How many people you reckon there are — white people, I mean — who would know his face if they seen it?"

Kelly shrugged. The idea seemed farfetched.

Joe Florey studied him intently, looking for acceptance of his notion and not finding it. "I'll admit it ain't likely. But through the years I've found out that when you're trailin' a man you better expect him to do what's unlikely." He looked down the creek. "We'll see after the likely first. This creek runs south a little ways more, then it cuts east. If he did go down the creek he wouldn't stay in it long after it changes direction. We'll ride that far and see if we find where he came out."

Joe took the west side of the creek bank. That seemed the most likely place for Fernandez to come out, eventually. Kelly took the east side. This gave him the double responsibility of watching for tracks and guarding against ambush. The two men rode to the point where the creek changed to an easterly course, and to give the effort its proper good measure they rode an extra mile beyond. But Kelly could tell, watching the old man across the creek, that Joe was rapidly losing his doubt; he was convinced the Mexican had gone up the creek. Kelly remained skeptical, but he said nothing when Joe Florey called a halt and reversed direction. The old man wasted no time getting back to the original crossing point; he loped his black horse.

When they had passed the original starting place, Florey rode into the creek, standing the black in the shallow middle of it while he studied both banks thoughtfully. He leaned way down on one side, peering through the nearly clear water to see if he could find any suspicious disturbance of the creek bottom. If there had been one the current had long since removed any trace.

"It's shallow all the way from here to the head of it," Florey said. "I'll ride in the creek where I can keep a sharp eye on both banks. You stay on top and don't let nobody shoot me."

Kelly said, "It'll be dark directly."

Sharply the old man demanded, "You think I'm too blind to see that? Hell, I seen the sun set twice as many times as you have. We'll ride as long as we can see."

There wasn't much tracking to it, Kelly thought, because there weren't any tracks. They traveled as fast as Joe's black horse could move through the shallow water at the edge of the creek. It was a tiring thing for a horse, but any tracks in this mud would be easy to see. If the fugitives had come this way, they hadn't left the water.

At dark Joe Florey had no choice but to stop. They had no food, either of them, and now Kelly regretted not sharing in that meal the possemen cooked at the Fernandez place. His stomach was beginning to protest. Joe Florey took a cut of tobacco from his pocket and trimmed off a piece with his pocketknife. He glanced at Kelly, considered a moment, then reluctantly offered Kelly the plug. "It ain't like a meal, but it takes the edge off a man's hunger."

Kelly shook his head. That was one habit he had gotten along without.

Joe stuck the plug back into his pocket and turned away. His momentary lapse was over; the old shell rehardened. In a little while he was asleep. Kelly sat up a long time, thinking of Griff, thinking of Tommie, wondering how she was bearing up without him, facing her two big problems alone. He would give a hundred dollars to be with her.

They were up with the daylight and moving again. Kelly wondered about Fernandez, where and how he had spent the night. He wondered if Fernandez too was hungry, or if he had something with him to eat.

Damn, but a pot of Tommie's coffee would taste good right now.

They had ridden more than an hour when Joe Florey suddenly reined up, shouting. Indifferent to getting his boots wet, the old man swung down and walked along in the creek, hunched over and looking at the mud along the bank. The tracks were so plain that Kelly could have spotted them, and he didn't claim to be a professional at trailing.

Joe Florey was grinning a little at first, until he got a grip on himself. Kelly saw relief in the heavy-browed eyes. It came to him as a surprise to realize that Florey had been doubting himself all along. Now his hunch had been vindicated. The pinched shoulders seemed to straighten a little. Joe said, "Same two horses, Barnhill's mare and the one the woman was ridin'. I reckon that Mexican decided it was safe now to come out of the creek. Figured there wouldn't none of them dumb gringos ever think of ridin' this far north."

He seated himself on the ground and pulled off his boots to pour the water out. "I told you, Kelly. I told you, and all the time you thought I was wrong." He seemed, in his exhilaration, to have forgotten, or at least temporarily to have put aside his old antagonism.

"I never argued with you, Joe."

"Too old, they said. But that smart-aleck Willcox is off down south a-runnin' his butt off, and old Joe Florey's got his Mexican spotted up thisaway."

"Not spotted yet. He's still got the length of the night."

"He probably stopped too, at least awhile. That shortens it some."

Kelly found it easier to forget his stomach now that they

had a solid trail to follow. It was a fairly easy trail in the main, for Fernandez seemed to be doing little now to hide it. Evidently he had felt confident after riding so far upstream.

You just keep on feeling that way, Kelly thought grimly, *and you'll soon be one caught Mexican.*

After a long time they broke out of the mesquite and came in view of a little farmhouse. Kelly knew from the look of it that it was probably a Mexican renter place; it had the earmarks of poverty about it. The tracks seemed to lead straight to it. Kelly drew up to study the place. "If we ride right on in there," he said uneasily, "we'll make a target for whoever's in the house."

Florey nodded thoughtfully. "The tracks are old; they were made yesterday. Even if he spent the night here he's probably gone."

"You said it yourself, always expect them to do the unlikely."

"Not that unlikely. You can stay here if you want to; I got me a trail to follow." Florey touched spurs gently to the black and rode on. Kelly had no choice but to catch up. He held his rifle tightly.

Before they reached the little frame house, Kelly saw a horse standing in a pen beside a crude brush-roofed shed thirty yards beyond. He pointed, and Florey nodded. "I see it."

They skirted the house, Kelly warily watching the windows for movement. Florey rode up to the fence, waved his hat and shouted. The horse shied away from him and trotted to the far end of the pen. Without getting out of the saddle, Florey took a good look at the prints the horse had just left.

"Same one, all right. That's the horse the woman was ridin'."

"Either she changed horses or she's still here."

Florey spat a brown stream as his gaze cut around. "That's the way I'd make it. Ain't but one way to find out, is there?"

They rode back around the same way they had come,

staying fifty or sixty feet out away from the house. Florey stopped in front. Kelly rode a little farther and dismounted, standing behind Griff's big dun horse. He gave Joe Florey time to get down, then he shouted.

"Whoever's in that house, come on out!"

He thought he could hear feet moving on the wooden floor, but he could not be sure. He called, "Come on out with your hands up!" He repeated it in the best Spanish he had.

Joe Florey laid his rifle across the saddle and took slow aim. The rifle roared, and a bullet cut through the tin chimney with a loud noise. Almost immediately a voice called from within the house.

"Do not shoot again!" it said in Spanish. "We are coming."

An old gray-haired man appeared in the doorway, his arms raised high. Behind him, cringing in fear, came two women, one old and one young.

"Anybody else?" Kelly demanded.

The old man said, "No one else. Just us. Just the three of us."

Kelly said, "You keep the rifle on them, Joe. I'll go in and see." He motioned for the three to step away from the door and give him room. Rifle ready, he paused a moment outside, listening, then rushed through the door.

The old man had told the truth; no one was here. Kelly walked back outside. He looked at the people, decided they had no weapons and motioned for them to lower their hands. Joe Florey came up, leading his horse.

Kelly asked, "Joe, how's your Spanish?"

"Damn sight better'n yours, I expect." Florey got right down to business. "We followed the tracks of two horses. They came right to this house, and one of the horses is still out there in the corral." His gaze lighted on the young woman. "You rode him?"

She began to sob. She could not have answered him if she tried.

The old man said, "This is my niece. Her husband was killed yesterday. Her brother-in-law brought her here."

Kelly asked, "Was his name Fernandez . . . Chacho Fernandez?"

The old man was trembling. "Yes. We knew nothing of this until he told us. My niece is without blame."

Kelly frowned. Maybe she was and maybe she wasn't. "Where is Chacho Fernandez now?"

The old man said he didn't know; Chacho had brought Dolores here and then had gone. Impatiently Kelly brought the rifle around and stuck the muzzle of it against the old man's flat belly. The two women cried out in fear. The old man trembled even more. He made two tries to speak before his voice finally came.

"In truth, sir, I do not know. I asked him, and he said it was better that I not know. He said I could not be forced to tell something if I did not know it."

Reluctantly Kelly began to decide the old man was telling the truth. Well, they could follow tracks again, like they had been doing. He had simply hoped they could short-cut the thing a bit.

He lowered the rifle. "You hungry, Joe?"

"I could eat."

Kelly told the old Mexican they had nothing to eat since yesterday and asked if there was anything in the house. The *viejo* sensed that they did not plan to kill him, and he half-wilted from relief. "Yes sir; yes sir," he said eagerly. "The women will prepare you something. There is still coffee from breakfast, and I have some *pulque*."

Kelly had tried Mexican *pulque* and had never found it to his liking. For one thing, it seemed they always kept it in a goatskin bag, and he had never brought himself to that degree of tolerance. But Joe Florey accepted the offer and turned up the goatskin, taking two long hard swallows before he lowered it. His face twisted from the fire of it, and he wiped his sleeve across his mouth.

"By God," he wheezed, "that has got authority!"

It was a poor house, and the fare was accordingly slim. But hunger made Kelly thankful for the goat stew and the red beans, rewarmed no telling how many times. The coffee was strong enough to blot out whatever shortcomings the food might have had.

Finished, Kelly pushed his chair back from the table and stared at the young woman. "Tell me what happened yesterday."

She cried fearfully, "I had nothing to do with it."

Fighting down his impatience, he began drawing the story out of her, going back two, three, and four times over some points that seemed to make little sense. That was the way things happened, more often than not. Things happened that shouldn't have, things that had no logical reason. Taking one turn they could come out comically. Taking another they could lead to tragedy.

As the woman's story unfolded painfully, Kelly could see the pattern of error compounded by error. He could see the senselessness of the whole affair.

"The mare," he pressed her. "Tell me again about the mare."

Dolores Fernandez repeated the story three times before he was satisfied with it. Chacho Fernandez, her brother-in-law, had been promised this good sorrel mare if he would break some broncs. He had talked of it so often she had become tired of hearing about it. He had been excited that morning as he and Felix had started for town with the broncs. At last he was going to own that mare.

Kelly clenched his fists in helpless fury.

Joe Florey said huskily, "That four-flushin' Barnhill. He's the one at the foot of all this."

Kelly shook his head. "That Mexican is still the one that pulled the trigger. But Barnhill set it all to movin'." Bitterly he ran his hand along the rifle. "It was in my mind when we started that I was goin' to kill that Mexican. I still will, if I get the chance. But I got me a good notion to blow a hole in that horse-trader, too."

Florey eyed him narrowly. Reproach was strong in his voice. "Talk is talk, and some people can do all of it they want to. But you can't. You're a Ranger. You can't afford it."

"A good man like Griffin Holliday, dead because of a

lyin' horse-trader and a quick-triggered Mexican! Somebody's got to pay."

Impatience quickened Florey's voice. "That's what we're here for. But there's a right way to see to it, and you better not forget. Else I'll leave you behind."

Kelly tried to draw the woman out some more, possibly to get an inkling of where Chacho Fernandez intended to go. Either she didn't know or she wouldn't tell . . . ever.

"We've found out all there is for us here," he said. "Let's travel."

Joe Florey walked to the door. He stopped there, swearing softly. "I thought we'd got rid of them," he grumbled. "I just wisht you'd look."

Odom Willcox was riding up with half a dozen posse-men, following the plain tracks left by Kelly and Joe. "Oh hell!" Kelly said and stepped outside.

Willcox dismounted and came up to the house, grinning in satisfaction. "Thought we'd catch up to you if we kept pushin'."

Kelly said, "You were goin' south, last we saw of you."

"Nobody ever did cut any sign. I got to thinkin'. I says to myself, old Joe Florey was always the foxy one. He seen somethin' he didn't want the rest of us to see, somethin' that told him to go north instead of south."

Irritably Joe said, "I seen nothin'. Just had a hunch, is all."

"Bet you had a hunch they'd get up a good reward."

Joe's face went red. "That's a damn lie!"

Willcox eyed him dubiously, not knowing whether he had hit the mark or not. "Well, there is a reward posted, and it'll likely grow before this is over. Albert Stout caught up to us this mornin'. They've spread an alarm all over South Texas. There's posses out today from here to the Rio Grande. Only, he ain't between here and the Rio Grande, is he? All the time you knew he was to the north of us."

For a moment Kelly thought he might have to step between the two men, but Willcox backed off in deference to Joe's years and his reputation. Age and experience had to be respected, even if not agreed with. Odom transferred his attention to the woman and the old couple. "Who are them Mexicans? They been hidin' him out or somethin'?"

Kelly explained that the woman had been a witness to the shooting, that her husband was the one they had found dead on the porch.

Willcox nodded stiffly. "Run as far as she could go, did she? She tell you where he's runnin' to?"

"She doesn't know."

"Like hell she don't." Willcox moved threateningly toward the Mexicans. "Them damn people, they always know more than they'll tell. I know how to get it out of them."

Kelly grabbed his arm and pulled him up short. "Willcox!" His voice was quiet, but it carried a threat. "They've told us all they know."

Willcox turned half around, challenge in his eyes. "You can't be sure. Time I get through with them we'll be sure."

Kelly's hand went tighter on the deputy's arm. "Seems to me like we've already crossed your county line."

Willcox didn't want to, but he admitted that was true.

"Well, then, you've got no more jurisdiction here than anybody else. Except me. I'm a *state* officer. So if you want to ride along with us you'll do what I tell you. Otherwise go on back; we don't want you."

Willcox stared at the Mexicans and muttered resentfully, but he had no good argument. His hands flexed in anger. Kelly figured he would like to have gotten them on that young woman. Willcox sank a couple more notches in Kelly's estimation.

Someone in the posse raised a protest. Kelly looked up and saw the trader Barnhill. Barnhill said, "You got no right, Sadler. Odom's an officer, duly appointed, and this is an emergency. County lines don't mean a damn in an emergency."

Kelly's anger, stirred by Willcox, began rising rapidly at the sight of the horse-trader. "Barnhill," he said, "I'm glad you're here, because I've got somethin' for you." He reached up and grabbed Barnhill's shirtfront and gave it a hard wrench. Barnhill tumbled to the ground. Crying out in surprise and rage, he made a reach for his pistol. He stopped himself just in time. Kelly's rifle barrel was pressed firmly against his teeth.

"You go on," Kelly seethed. "You just reach for that pistol. I'll spatter your damn brains all over this yard!"

There was murder in Kelly Sadler's eyes, and Barnhill could see it. The color drained from the trader's face as he lay there, afraid to move, afraid even to breathe. Fear built in him until he could stand it no longer, then he turned over, and threw up whatever he had had to eat. Kelly backed away but kept the rifle pointed at him, in case Barnhill did something in foolish desperation. Kelly hoped he would.

The posse watched in shocked silence and surprise. Finally Albert Stout came cautiously to the front. "Kelly," he spoke experimentally, "Kelly, take the gun off him. Kelly. . . ."

The tall man was shaking a little, and it took all the nerve he had. But Kelly turned to look at him, and he had to yield. He respected Albert. Sure, Albert had his shortcomings, but they were honest ones; he always did the best he was able. For Albert, Kelly backed away.

Albert's voice quavered a little, and Kelly knew the effort he was making. "This ain't no time or place for us to be killin' one another. We're all here for the same purpose to get the man that killed Griff."

Kelly pointed his chin at the trader, hunched on hands and knees, still sick. "It was Barnhill that killed Griff."

Albert blinked and looked at the other possemen a moment. "Now, Kelly, you know that can't be so. I was there."

"He didn't pull the trigger, but he as good as loaded the gun." He told what the Mexican woman had related.

Odom Willcox said, "Them Mexicans will all lie. She told you that to protect the man who done the killin."

"No, she told the truth. Griff figured it was that way all along."

Albert Stout sat on the ground, tears streaming down his cheeks. Kelly had told about the mistake in translation that led to the drawing of guns. The tall posseman rubbed his rough hand over his face. "I never claimed to be an interpreter. I always tried to get Griff to hire him a good Mexican for that."

Joe Florey put his hand on Albert's shoulder. "Griff always liked you, Albert. He liked havin' you with him. That's why he wouldn't hire somebody else. You' always did your best."

"I got Griff killed."

Kelly said, "Nobody is goin' to blame you, Albert, so there's no point in you blamin' yourself. But I do blame a man who told a lie, and sent a good man out to die on account of it." He turned back to Barnhill. "Get up from there!"

Barnhill pushed to his feet. The possemen had all drawn back from him; he was standing alone. Suddenly he didn't have a friend.

Kelly said, "I don't know how long this hunt will take. It could be over with today or it could go on for a week. But whenever it's over I'll come lookin' for you. If you're in Domingo when I get there, I'll kill you!"

Barnhill cringed like a whipped dog. Legs shaking, he managed to get onto his horse and pull it around. He took a last look at the posse, seeking a sympathetic face and finding none. He dug spurs into his horse's ribs and headed south in a lope that would kill the animal in five miles if he kept it up.

The Mexicans had watched, not comprehending any of it. A bunch of crazy gringos, trying to kill one another. But, *mala suerte*, they had not done so. Perhaps another time. . . .

Kelly waited until Barnhill was well gone before he took his eyes from him. He turned, finally, to Joe Florey. "You ready to start trackin' again?"

"I was ready while ago, when I got interrupted." He gave Odom Willcox a long, hard study. "I'd as soon go on by myself, but if you're bound to come, you stay the hell back out of my way and don't mess up no tracks. *Sabe?*"

Willcox nodded. "You find him, Joe, and we'll shoot him!"

Joe looked sharply at the men who accompanied Willcox, and the guns they carried. "Be damn careful you don't shoot yourselves."

Kelly mounted his horse and pulled it beside Willcox. "You be slow about startin' anything. I'm the one in authority here. If he's to be got, *I'll* get him."

Joe Florey was annoyed at all of them. "Time's runnin' on, and so is that Mexican. There won't anybody get him. Kelly Sadler, you can stay here and jaw with those hombres from now till dark if you want to, but I'm goin' on."

The old man's reproach brought Kelly up short. He hadn't intended to get in an argument with Willcox, but he would have if Joe hadn't spoken up. Kelly stayed back a little out of the way while the old Ranger rode a hundred yards northeast and then cut back at an angle, looking down. It took him only a minute to pick up the trail. He made no signal but abruptly pulled back and started north in a trot.

That was the way with those oldtimers, Kelly thought. They figured if you weren't smart enough to read their minds by their actions, then you didn't have any business tagging along; you would just be in the way anyhow. Kelly spurred to catch up but was careful to remain a little to the left of the hoofprints. Florey gave him hardly a glance, though he did look back to be sure Willcox and the others stayed at a respectful distance. Florey rode in silence a long time, chewing on problems of his own. At length he said, "A man who stands around and wastes his time arguin' with a fool ain't none too bright himself."

"He gets under my skin," Kelly admitted ruefully, knowing Joe was right.

"He'll do a damn sight more to that Mexican than get under his skin, ever he gets the chance. If you don't want Willcox to blow that hombre's guts all over two counties, you better see that he doesn't get to him before you do."

101

Joe spat. "There'll have to be an election to fill Griff's office. If we all bring that Mexican in alive to stand trial, everybody shares the honor. But if a man was able to go home and say that he was the one who killed the murderer of Griffin Holliday, he could beat Jeff Davis and Robert E. Lee without a runoff."

Joe let Kelly absorb that and added, "He's bloodthirsty, Odom is. He don't belong in Griff's office. There's a time to be tough and a time to be gentle. Odom Willcox can't tell them apart. Give him a chance and he'll leave dead Mexicans and maybe some gringos as well, scattered all over his county."

NINE

The rest of that day they followed the hoofprints. It was easy to tell where Chacho Fernandez had spent the night. The trail led to a windmill and for a time seemed hopelessly lost amid so many fresher tracks, made since Fernandez had passed. Joe Florey grumbled aloud about so many people riding around over the country without any business and messing up a good set of tracks. Eventually he found where Fernandez had set a course paralleling the trail but avoiding using it directly.

"He'd've been better off," Kelly observed, "to have stayed in the trail and let everybody else cover up his sign."

"Some of the riders who made these tracks might've been lookin' for *his*," Joe told him. "He done right." There was a touch of approval in his voice. "He's done pretty good all along."

Near sundown a small frame house showed up in a narrow valley half a mile away, but the trail showed no sign of angling down toward it. Joe found a spot where the tracks stirred a little, indicating that Fernandez had stopped and looked down in that direction, possibly contemplating riding there and then deciding against it. The tracks led on north.

Squinting, Kelly made out that someone was working in a cornfield near the house. He saw no point in riding down there and asking questions. Even if the people there had seen Fernandez, they probably could not tell any more about him than was made obvious by the tracks. But Odom Willcox didn't see it that way. He came up in a lope, demanding to know why they didn't ride to that house and look around. He didn't take Kelly's answer as having much validity. "Anyway," he said, "me and the boys are gettin' kind of lank. Ought to be somethin' down there a man could eat."

Joe Florey gave Kelly an impatient glance that said to let them go. The farther behind they were, the better Joe liked it. So Odom Willcox spurred off toward the frame house, all the posse trailing closely after him except Albert Stout. The tall deputy gravely watched them go and asked, "Be all right if I ride alongside of you awhile, Kelly? I wasn't hungry noways."

"Glad to have you, Albert."

Joe Florey made no objection. Kelly suspected that Joe would rather have Albert up here than Kelly anyway.

Albert said, "You ever had to listen to Odom talk for long at a time? He'd wear the ears off a blue-tick hound." He frowned. "You figurin' on takin' that Mexican alive?"

Kelly wasn't sure how to answer. "That depends on the Mexican."

"Then you better watch Odom. He figures to kill him any way he can."

Kelly glanced at Joe. The old man said nothing, but it must have gratified him to have his suspicions confirmed.

Albert told Kelly he had talked to Ranger headquarters by telephone and they had said for Kelly to stay on the trail as long as he thought was necessary.

"You see Tommie last night?" Kelly asked worriedly.

"I seen her. She was bearin' up well, I thought, considerin'."

"They buried Griff today, I reckon. I ought to've been with her."

"No, Kelly, you're where you belong."

The sun went down. Darkness was rapidly closing in when the posse came up from behind, riding hard. Odom Willcox whooped as he passed the three men. Joe Florey shouted angrily what they were doing to the tracks.

Odom said, "To hell with the tracks! We know where he's at!"

Florey cursed, but Kelly didn't waste time. He spurred to catch up to the deputy. Willcox said triumphantly, "Told you it wasn't no waste of time for us to go down there. We found us a nest of Mexicans that was tickled to death to tell us about our man."

"*What* about him?"

"That he's hidin' in a house a little ways up the road, or was a few hours ago. They figure he's apt to leave come dark, and we got to get there before he does."

Kelly thought of the damage they were doing to Fernandez' tracks. "Ever occur to you they might've lied to throw you off?"

"They didn't lie; we made damn sure of that."

Kelly could well imagine how Willcox had done it.

The deputy said, "We told them that if we found out they had lied, we'd come back and slit their throats for them, all the way from the old man right down to that good-lookin' girl of theirs. They didn't lie to us."

The possemen were like penned-up hounds turned loose on a fresh scent. It would be hard to get any order into this mission now, or to keep any if they ever got it.

Full darkness came before the house suddenly loomed up ahead.

"Slow down," Kelly demanded. "We'll overrun it."

"Hell yes we'll overrun it!" Willcox declared. "That's the whole idea; catch him before he can get away."

"We can't see him in the dark; we'll wind up shootin'

each other. We'll surround the house and keep him there till daylight. Then we'll take him."

"And let him sneak out on us? This is my deal now, Sadler. If you don't like it, stay out of it." Willcox seemed then to dismiss Kelly from consideration. He spoke to the others. "Come on, boys, we'll rush them. Anybody that's in there, they're helpin' him. Shoot anybody that moves!"

He spurred full-tilt toward the house, firing at the faint lamplight which showed through the windows. The rest of the men rode in with him. Even Albert Stout, for he had been caught up in the excitement. Kelly held back, and Joe Florey pulled up beside him.

Kelly said, "That's a damnfool thing they're doin'."

"You told him that?"

"I told him."

"That's all you can do then, unless you shoot him yourself."

It sounded for a moment like the Civil War all over again as the horsemen spurred toward the house, firing. The lamplight suddenly winked out, and from a window came answering fire, flashing in the darkness. Just one gun, as far as Kelly could tell, but it was a big one.

His heart sank a little. *They'll get him,* he thought. *They'll kill everybody that's in the house . . . man, woman, and child.*

All for the glory of Odom Willcox.

The riders wavered a little at the flash of the rifle in the window. Some rode on around, circling the house in the darkness. They kept up the fire, and Kelly heard a couple of half-spent slugs whistle by him.

"Good God!" he exclaimed, swinging to the ground and grabbing at the reins to keep the frightened horse from running away. "If that Mexican doesn't kill them all, they'll kill each other!"

He knew what it would be like there now in the darkness. They were firing excitedly at anything which moved, and that probably included their fellow possemen. He had seen it happen before. "Goddamn fool Willcox!" Kelly shouted, more to himself than to Florey. "I ought to've killed him."

"You may not have to," Joe said. He had also dismounted and was standing behind his horse for protection from stray bullets. A man did not like to expose his horse needlessly, but better the horse than himself.

The firing slowed and finally stopped. Kelly could hear shouting as the possemen tried to locate one another. He could hear a woman crying in the house, calling out in Spanish for mercy.

Kelly said, "I'm gettin' up there, Joe. They'll kill everybody that's left." He loped in, shouting to let the possemen know who he was. Even so, he bent low to avoid furnishing a good target.

He found the possemen scattered around the house, still calling to one another in an effort to get everyone located. A Mexican woman stood on the porch, crying hysterically that her husband and son were dead, begging not to be killed herself, begging for no more shooting.

Kelly called, "Everybody hold your fire! Next man fires a gun, I'll kill him myself."

He heard Odom Willcox somewhere out toward a shed. "That you, Sadler? Be careful. We got us a den of rattlesnakes here."

Rifle on the ready, Kelly dismounted near the house, stepping behind the horse again until he could get a good idea where everybody was, who they were. In Spanish he called. "You people at the house . . . come on out this way with your hands up!"

A woman came down off the little porch, sobbing uncontrollably. A much younger woman — a girl, actually — followed her, her hands up to her face in mute fear. "My son. . . ." the woman cried. "My husband . . . they are in there, dead."

Kelly could still see movement in the house. "Come on out here, the rest of you!"

He saw what he thought was an old man, judging by the way he moved. He staggered out the door, hunched over, evidently badly wounded.

Kelly demanded, "How many more inside?"

The old man cursed him in the foulest Spanish Kelly had ever heard. "My son and my grandson," he shouted in such a rage that his voice lifted and broke and started again at a lower level. "One is dead and the other is wounded so that he may be dying. You *rinches* . . . you damned *rinches*. . . ." He managed somehow to shake a fist and came down off the porch, trying to rush at Kelly in his fury. But his forward movement carried him off balance. He stumbled and fell.

Old man or not, he could be dangerous. Kelly stuck the muzzle of his rifle in the man's face to tell him he had better just lie there awhile. "We are looking for Chacho Fernandez. Is he inside?"

"Go to hell, you damned dirty *rinches!*"

Odom Willcox had come around from the other side afoot, in a rage. He grabbed the old man by the front of his shirt and jerked him halfway to his feet.

"Tell us where Chacho Fernandez is or I'll blow your head off."

He was so angry he forgot to try to speak in Spanish.

Kelly said, "Easy, the old man's been shot."

"He'll be shot a lot worse if he don't talk."

Kelly voice hardened. "I said *easy*. Let him down."

The woman dropped to her knees beside the old man. She cried out, "He is old. Do not kill him."

Kelly asked her, "Where is Chacho Fernandez?"

"He is gone."

The old man angrily told the woman to shut up, to tell the damned *rinches* nothing. But she was far more interested in saving what was left of her family than in placating the old man. "He left awhile ago, before you came."

Kelly asked, "Where did he go?"

The old man grabbed the woman's arm and shook her violently. "Be quiet, woman."

She said, "I do not know where he went. I did not want to know."

Kelly was uncertain whether to believe her. He looked at the house, a vague black mass in the darkness. "He *could* still be in there."

Willcox grunted. "I say we better be safe. I say burn the house. If he's in there he'll come out."

Kelly pointed his chin at the old man. "He says there's somebody in there wounded."

"Let him come out or let him burn up. I don't much give a damn."

"You want to go in and look?" Kelly asked Willcox, knowing the answer would be a firm negative. "Then I'll go. You-all cover me."

Willcox cautioned, "Don't expect me to go in there with you."

"I sure wouldn't expect that," Kelly replied, a little gravel in his voice.

Willcox had called it right; Kelly had the same feeling walking up onto that porch and facing that dark door that he would have going into a rattlesnake den. His hands were sweaty on the riflestock. He paused, then took a running start that carried him into the house and across the room in three long strides. He ran into some kind of small table and knocked it over with a great clatter and smashing of dishes. He turned with his back to the far wall, rifle aimed at two shapes lying on the floor. One of them appeared to be trying to move. "Hold still or I'll kill you!" Kelly declared in Spanish. The only answer was a groan. Kelly studied the room until he was satisfied with it, then stepped into an adjoining small room and, in turn, a lean-to. He kicked over a wooden bed to be sure no one was under it.

He walked back to the door and called. "It's all clear. I'll light a lamp if I can find one."

He struck a match and looked around. He found a lamp lying on the floor, its glass chimney smashed, half of its oil spilled out. He kicked some broken plates and cups aside, stood the small table aright, and placed the lamp on it. Without a protective chimney the light flickered badly and was in constant danger of going out.

He saw that the walls were splintered in many places where bullets had smashed through the clapboard siding. On the floor by the front window lay a rifle, a cartridge jammed in the breech. It was the only firearm he could see. If it hadn't become jammed, and if everybody in the house hadn't been killed, the fight might still be going on . . . if a man wanted to call it a fight. It had been terribly one-sided.

He knelt to examine the groaning man and found him to be actually only a boy, hit deep in the shoulder and still bleeding, past the point of knowing what was going on around him. The other man — roughly middle-aged — was dead. Odom Willcox and a couple of other men cautiously entered the house, crouching, guns ready in nervous hands.

"This ain't Chacho Fernandez," Kelly said. "God knows where *he* is."

Willcox trembled a little now in the aftermath of the excitement. "They're all guilty. They harbored him."

Kelly wondered how guilty the boy was, and said so.

Willcox declared. "Boy's old enough to shoot a gun and kill a man. Them Mexicans, they train them young."

A commotion stirred outside. A couple of men came in, carrying someone. They laid the body carefully on the wooden floor.

Kelly's mouth dropped open. "Albert!"

Albert Stout lay still, his face gone to the color of ash. Kelly didn't have to touch him to know he was dead.

One of the possemen declared, "I seen him when he fell from his horse out yonder by the shed. He was dead when I got to him."

Odom Willcox cursed. "Damn Mexicans! I say hang every one of them!"

Kelly was too stunned to say anything. But Joe Florey wasn't. He said, "It wasn't Mexicans killed him, it was one of you!"

Odom Willcox turned in fury. He cursed Joe Florey as a stupid, senile old man. "Which one of us would've killed a good man like Albert Stout?"

"Any of you, the way you come ridin' in here in a wild sashay like that, shootin' like a bunch of wild Indians. The only fire that ever come from the house was through that front window. That one old rifle, I expect, was the only gun they had. It never at no time fired in the direction of that shed out back."

Willcox refused to accept it, but gradually Kelly saw belief come into the faces of the other possemen. Belief and a desperate remorse.

It was one of Joe Florey's weaknesses that when he knew he was right he couldn't resist rubbing salt into someone else's sores. "Somebody's got to take Albert back to Domingo now and go tell his wife that she's a widow, and tell her Albert died because of a bunch of damn chuckleheads, led by the champion damn chucklehead of them all!" Pretty soon he had them as angry as they were grieved.

Kelly knew he had better shut Joe off before they all went to the fists right here in this little house, with two dead men and a badly wounded boy lying at their feet. "Stop it, all of you! One bad mistake don't have to bring on another. "

Someone brought in the old man and the two women. Willcox shouted, "I say we kill them all!"

"Would that help?" Kelly demanded.

"It'd help pay for Albert."

The old Mexican looked at the body of the deputy and turned in anger toward Kelly. "Where are the rest of them? Where are the other *rinches* I killed?"

"You killed nobody," Kelly replied curtly. "One of us killed this one by mistake."

"You lie! I killed this one, and I killed many more. You are hiding them out there in the darkness to rob me."

"Hush, old man. There are some here who would kill you in a minute. Don't give them reason."

"Kill me, then! Shoot me! Hang me! My people will know I died fighting the gringos, and that I took many of them to hell with me!"

Kelly looked worriedly at the possemen. Most of them savvied enough Spanish to get the gist of what this wild-eyed old man was saying. If he didn't shut him up there wouldn't be a live Mexican left on the place, not even the women. He doubled his fist and drove it into the stubbled chin as hard as he could. The old man fell back against the splintered wall, then sank unconscious. The older of the two women cried out and dropped to her knees beside him.

Kelly looked first at the old man, then at Willcox. *Fanatics!* Goddamned fanatics! The world might eventually find peace if it didn't always have these fanatics on every side, building fires where there had been none and fanning them until they became conflagrations!

TEN

Chacho Fernandez had no way of knowing the tremendous forces he had set loose, for he was traveling alone, avoiding both friend and foe because of fear that he could not tell one from the other.

It was a hard time for the Mexican population of South Texas, particularly for male Mexicans moving across country where they were not personally known. Any one of them might be Chacho Fernandez, the Anglo possemen feared, so to be on the safe side they stopped and arrested just about any Mexican who could not instantly be identified. If he made some suspicious move, they clubbed him. If it was not safe or convenient to club him, they shot him.

It was generally believed that the shooting of Sheriff Griffin Holliday was part of a conspiracy, no doubt related to the vigorous action he had taken against the horsethief rings. So in the press Chacho Fernandez was identified as one of the ringleaders, and any Mexican who could not account for himself was regarded as a probable member of the gang. It was suspected by some that in his flight he had gathered a large number of his confederates around him and that they were making a sweep across the southern part of Texas.

At Seguin one Mexican was shot and another hanged for refusing to give information which he did not have. At Ottine a suspect was fatally wounded. At Willow Springs another man ran from a posse and was brought down.

Declared a San Antonio newspaper: "The fact that three of them have hung, one to death and two others to unconsciousness, and that they emphatically refused to give any information shows that they have regard for neither death nor punishment."

At San Diego one Mexican was killed and another captured by Rangers, who later determined that neither was Fernandez. Said the San Antonio paper: "They were probably horsethieves."

In the Mexican *jacales* the people laid low, getting out no more than they had to. In the old town plazas men talked glowingly of Chacho Fernandez and how he had aroused the gringos like no man since Cortina, or perhaps even since Santa Anna. They discussed the improbability of his escape from these hundreds of gringo possemen scouring the country, and in the churches people lighted candles for him and prayed that the good Lord would see fit to bring him safely across the river into sanctuary. In the cantinas men were beginning to make up songs about him in the old way of the Mexican people, the spontaneous *corridos* that always spring up immediately upon some unusual event, upon some display of great heroism.

114

Even as he ran, Chacho Fernandez was becoming known among his own people as a hero ten feet tall, spurring the sorrel mare and holding the reins in his teeth and firing two pistols at once, laughing as he shot down *cherifes* and *rinches* the way the scythe cuts the weeds, felling them by the dozens before him, the mare trampling their bodies as she carried him safely away. In a week, from San Antonio to Rio Grande City on the river, he was a legend.

And he was still at large, working his way inexorably south.

Running was hardly the word, for to have run would have been to betray himself to the gringos scattered across this country like the cactus and the centipedes and the rattlesnakes. Always, it seemed, he could see them in front of him, to the side of him, behind him in singles or twos, or groups from three to a dozen. There was hardly a period of more than an hour or two in which he saw nobody. He had thought at first it would be safer to travel at night, but this he had given up because twice he had almost ridden into a nest of *rinches* before he realized it. Once they had begun firing at him in the darkness. All that saved him was that one of their party had walked off into the brush to answer a midnight call of nature, and he thought they were mistakenly shooting at him. He had called for the firing to stop and then had hurried into the camp, holding up his britches and cursing them for being twelve brands of damn fools. Chacho had taken advantage of the distraction to ease away in the darkness. He had not seen the man out there, and evidently the man had not seen him.

Daylight travel increased his chance of being seen, but it also gave him a better chance to see.

He found it hard to believe all these people were after him. He kept wondering if some truly great tragedy might have occurred, or if perhaps a war had begun that he had not heard about. Times, when he was in sight of a place that appeared to be lived in by Mexican people, he longed to go there and see what he could find out. But he dared not.

Even if they did not turn him in, he might bring upon them the same kind of trouble he had unwittingly brought upon the Bustamantes.

He kept moving, eating sparingly of what the Bustamantes had given him. A couple of times he borrowed from empty houses he came across.

The Bustamantes. They never crossed his mind without

starting anew a terrible anxiety. If he had had anything to give, short of his life, he would have given it to know the outcome of the shooting he had heard as he was leaving there the second night of his flight. Was anybody dead there? Or . . . and the thought always chilled him . . . was anybody still alive?

He would bet that old Esteban was dead. The *viejo* would have kept shooting until there was no life left in him to pull a trigger. He was a man of war, that one, and where there was no war he was always ready to make one. He would have welcomed death, even courted it, if he could go down fighting the enemy rather than to wither away of old age and die ingloriously of some child's disease. War had been life to him; age and inactivity had been a form of death.

Chacho treated the sorrel mare with great care, conserving her strength as much as he could. But by the end of the third day he knew she would never be able to carry him all the way to the river. He could feel her weakening under him. A night's rest helped some, but in the morning she was not as strong as she had been the morning before. The spring grass did not yet have the strength needed for this kind of riding, and there was no grain.

It seemed that for every mile he rode south, he rode two either east or west, staying in the heavier brush, avoiding the men he could see looking for him. At times when his trail was too clear, he would double back on it a way, then strike off at a tangent, hoping to confuse and slow down anyone who might be trailing him.

The fourth day he came to a barbed wire fence, one of far too many which had crossed his path. He had no pliers to cut them with, so he jerked the steeples from three adjacent posts by tying his maguey rope to the wires. He pushed the wires down as near the ground as the slack would allow and held them with his foot while the mare gingerly stepped across, rolling her nose in anxiety. She greatly feared the wire. The only blemishes he had found had been old cuts, long since healed, on both of her forefeet. As a filly she had probably become entangled, leaving her with a dread of sharp, cold barbs.

This fourth day she shied a little while crossing the fence, and she cut her right hind foot. Cursing the bad luck, he let the wires spring up behind her. He patted her rump, talking calmly to her, ran his hand gently down her hind leg and then picked up the foot. She flinched, for it stung. The blood was running. He could tell it was deep enough to become a problem, but not enough at this point to cripple her.

If he were at home he could clean it, stop the blood, rub meat grease into the wound, and tie something around it to help keep the dirt and the flies out. But here he had nothing.

Riding, he kept looking down at the foot, kept watching the mare's stride to see if she might be starting to favor the limb. It was no surprise to him that she did, a little.

"I am sorry, *maqui*," he said, "to have brought you to this."

Thirst was beginning to plague him. He had not had a drink of water all day, nor had the mare. He had known of a good waterhole this morning, but he had been forced to pass it by. Three gringos were camped there.

He sliced open a green prickly pear leaf, hoping he might suck enough juice out of the pulp inside to help him, but the taste gagged him.

Damn rinches, they are like the heelflies, buzzing all around. He had seen heelflies drive cattle into a frenzy, forcing them to run aimlessly in a vain effort to shake them away. *They are trying to do that to me, to make me break and run and let them get me.*

117

He began pulling tiny mesquite leaves, fresh and green, sucking them to help bring up the saliva, taking care not to bite into them because of the bitter flavor that came out when the leaf was ruptured. But this was no real answer. He had to have water, not only for himself but for the mare.

He knew where he was, and he knew that three, maybe

four miles to the south and west was a windmill. He remembered the water as being a bit on the gyppy side, but at a time like this it would taste sweeter than wine, and far better than old Esteban's pulque. He headed in that direction, pausing a moment to take a long look behind him. He watched ahead and on both sides of him as he rode. He sucked on the green leaves and tried not to think of water, for the thought was more painful than pleasurable.

Soon he could see the big old cypress fan standing high above the brush-covered skyline. That was the hell of it in this country—a windmill always looked nearer than it was because a man could see it so far. That made it very difficult to keep his mind from his thirst.

It did not distract him so badly that he failed to see the men. He caught a faint movement, far ahead of him, and it set off an electric sensation in his spine. He stopped, squinting in the sun's glare.

Damn them! There must have been half a dozen horsemen over in the direction of that mill.

He hoped they were riding through. From appearances they were riding in almost the same direction that he was. But as he drew closer to the mill he could see they had dismounted around it. Presently he saw a thin wisp of smoke. They had built a fire, probably to cook something to eat.

As late as it was now, if that was the case, they would not move on any more today. By the time they got something fixed for a late dinner or an early supper—whichever it was—they would almost certainly camp for the night, near the water.

Damn them, and damn them again!

There was no way he could slip in to the water with so many men camped on it.

He studied the windmill with a vast regret and turned away from it, keeping the heavy brush between it and himself. Somewhere, surely, there must be a watering place they had not yet covered. Studying, he remembered a dirt tank to the south. Some gringo rancher had built it in the edge of a draw, using mules and slips and fresnoes and some Mexican sweat to hollow out a depression, dragging up the dirt from the bottom and piling it on the far side to create a tiny dam. In rainy times when runoff water coursed down the draw, a little of it would be impounded in the tank, on deposit against the dry times that invariably came.

Chacho recalled that the last time he had seen the tank the water was almost green from having stood so long without being flushed, without being replenished by fresh runoff. On that occasion he had not been thirsty enough to consider drinking it. But a man's standards had to change with altered circumstances. A hatful of green water right now would be worth a hard month's wages.

There was no windmill at the site to serve as a pointer; he had to take the direction on memory and instinct. If he could strike within a mile or so of it, the converging cattle trails would lead him. If he missed by a couple of miles, he had as well miss by twenty.

He felt the mare tiring beneath him. She still favored that hind foot, though not enough yet that he could class her as lame. He knew by the set of her mouth that she was as thirsty as he was. He couldn't ride her this way forever, not without water.

He found the cattle trails easily. For one thing, he encountered cattle plodding along them, going to water in the late afternoon. As he approached they shied away and left the trail to him. After he passed they stopped, staring after him, uncertain about going on to water with a horseman in front of them.

Chacho noted the brand on the cattle, a Double N, and tried to remember whose it was. He guessed he had never known, for no ranch name or individual owner came to mind. Like many cowboys, Anglo as well as Mexican, Chacho could read very little of words on paper, but he had learned early in life to read brands. He knew most of the letters of the alphabet not because they had been taught him from a book but because he had learned them from the hide of a cow.

Ahead he saw a heavy clump of mesquite, a jungle of

growth. That would be the tanksite. The tenacious mesquite tree must have been in this land ever since the day God had finished it and called it good. In a hostile environment it sent its roots deeper than any other plant, searching always for any trace of water, finding it and thriving where no other type of tree could survive except the huisache and creosote and other scrubbier forms. Given an opportunity like a fairly constant hole of water, and disturbed earth in which to find a seedbed, it would flourish and multiply with unbelievable rapidity. Chacho would guess this surface tank was no more than ten or fifteen years old. In that short space of time, mesquites by the hundreds had come up around it, all stealing water.

That jungle would shield him once he reached the tank. But what if it were shielding someone already there? If some gringo possemen were waiting there, he would not see them until he had ridden out across the opening between this final outlying thicket and that dense stand around the water. It would be too late then to turn away from danger.

Running his tongue over dry lips, he dismounted to get some strength back into his legs and to let the mare rest a bit without his weight upon her back. Mostly, though, he dismounted to take time to watch, to study.

It was difficult. The afternoon's heat and the cruel thirst seemed to impair his sight. He blinked. It would clear momentarily, but before he could fasten his attention on any one thing the swimminess would come back. He rubbed his eyes in a vain effort to clear them. But he could not reach the real trouble; it was on the inside.

The mare saw first. She picked up her ears and turned her head a little. Chacho squinted, searching for whatever had caught her attention. He thought at first that she had simply seen a cow, but as he watched the cow cleared and sharpened and became a horse. On that horse sat a man, riding into the brush. Chacho cursed violently in a moment of wild anger. Then he got hold of himself and turned his ear in that direction, listening intently. He thought he could hear, very faintly, the light sound of laughter on the thin June breeze.

This one, too, he thought bitterly. *We'll have to go on.*

But he looked at the mare, standing drooped, her mouth open, saliva dripping from the bits. She couldn't make another waterhole. Neither, he thought, could he.

We've got to get water here. But how?

A cow bawled, somewhere behind him. He turned, looking, and he saw a chance. At best, a thin one, but a chance. He remounted the mare, touched spurs gently to her sides and rode a wide circle around the cattle. In the distance of about a mile he picked up thirty or thirty-five cows and a couple of bulls, and perhaps fifteen or twenty calves. He threw them into a small herd and started pushing them toward the tank. Some of the calves became separated from their mothers and started bawling. The cows would answer back and look around anxiously for their offspring.

The herd announced itself long before it ever reached the tank. That was just as well, Chacho thought. The men at the water would not expect a fugitive to make this much noise. He took the pistol from its prominent place in his waistband and shoved it into the same place beneath the shirt, where it would not be so obvious.

His heartbeat quickened as the cattle went into the heavy thicket. He had to fight a wild impulse to pick up and run. He saw three men swing onto their horses and pull back away from the water. They were range men; they knew better than to block a waterhole when somebody was bringing in livestock.

Chacho shouted and whistled at the cattle, trying to look as if he did this every day for a living. He waved at the first rider and spoke to him genially in Spanish. The gringo answered in a friendly manner and fell in behind without being asked, helping Chacho push the cattle on to water.

The other men pulled back out of the way and watched interestedly. Trying not to appear overanxious, Chacho found a fresh place along the edge of the tank where the cattle had not yet stirred the water. He stepped to the ground, loosened the girth and let the mare drink. He flopped on his belly, brushed a little dirty film off the water and began slaking a long day's thirst.

He didn't even notice, until after he had taken all he thought was safe, that the water did indeed have a green cast to it.

He heard one of the men on horseback say in English, "Damn Mexicans will drink anything."

"So would I," another replied, "if I was thirsty enough. I reckon he's followed them cows and eaten their dust all day."

Chacho eyed them warily but tried not to look concerned. He rubbed his sleeve across his mouth and waited a little, figuring to let the first drink settle and then take another. One of the possemen asked him who he worked for and he told him the Double N. He hoped none of these men did, or they would know he didn't belong. He held his breath as one of the other men took a close look at the mare, remarking that she looked like a good one. Chacho told him the patron had recently bought the mare for his daughter but wanted Chacho to ride her awhile to be sure she would not pitch. That would account for the mare's not having the Double N brand.

"How far are you going with the cattle?" the first posseman asked.

"To the next pasture only," said Chacho. "I need to be done before sundown."

He was less thirsty this time and less in a frenzy to drink. He took a little more care in brushing back the film and the remnants of drowned insects, catching the cleanest water he could on the brim of his hat and drinking it that way. A man's own hat was not considered unsanitary.

The cattle and the mare had finished. Chacho tightened the girth, swung into the saddle and started gathering the cattle. A couple of the possemen helped him throw them together. They reined up at the edge of the thicket and waved as he moved on south, driving the cattle.

He held his breath and tried to stay busy with the cattle

until he was well out of sight. He tried not to keep looking back over his shoulder. But every so often he had to do it, afraid any minute he would see them coming after him.

They never did. As soon as he thought it was safe, he left the cattle and rode on south, considerably refreshed, feeling the mare stepping a little more sprightly beneath him.

But the fifth day he knew she was done. The wound was swelling and making pus. She was favoring that foot considerably. He started looking anxiously for other horses so that he could make a swap, but he found none. By noon he knew she had gone as far as she would be able to carry him. He got off and led her awhile, and watched the limp get worse.

He sighed, finally, and resigned himself to the inevitable. He led her up to a heavy thicket, took off the saddle and dropped it to the ground. His eyes burned as he looked at the mare and gently patted her neck. "Little *maqui*, you have done better by me than I deserved. Another horse would have quit me days ago. I hope I have not crippled you for life."

He thought once of Luisa Aguilar, for whom he had taken the mare in the first place, and realized this was the first time all day she had crossed his mind. "She did not deserve you, little *maqui*. And neither did I." He slipped the bridle from her head and waved his hands with a sudden violence. "Go! You are free now."

She trotted off a few steps and turned to watch him, not quite comprehending.

Chacho hid the saddle and blanket as best he could in the brush. He kept the rope and the bridle, hoping he might chance across a horse somewhere that he could catch; he could always ride bareback if he had to. He flung the saddlebags over his shoulder, took a last loving look at the sorrel mare, then turned his face south again.

Afoot.

ELEVEN

Joe Florey sat sipping at black coffee while Kelly Sadler fried strips of bacon in a small pan over a modest campfire in the dark of the summer night. They accepted provisions wherever they found them, from ranchers, from posses they came across. The bacon and coffee had been given them earlier in the day by a handful of deputies who had overtaken them, hoping they might be Chacho Fernandez and some confederate. Kelly had noticed one thing different about this particular posse: it included several Mexicans.

The long zigzag course had carried them down into what was commonly called the border country. There were far more Mexican people here as a percentage of the total population than was the case northward around Domingo. Here they made up an important political force. There were even Mexican sheriffs, something unheard of in the northern counties, where Mexicans were sometimes not even permitted to vote, much less to hold office. If these men were any less diligent than the Anglo officers in their search for Chacho Fernandez, Kelly could not tell it.

Odom and the other possemen had left Kelly and Joe days ago, moving on south to be where the action was. "You-all never will catch him, pokin' along here followin' cold tracks like a pair of turtles," he had said. "You'll still be ploddin' when we've shot him into mincemeat."

"You're supposed to catch him, not kill him," Joe Florey had grumped. "He's supposed to be tried in court as a warnin' to others."

Willcox had declared, "A dead man is a pretty good warnin'." He had ridden away, taking three men with him. The rest had disbanded after the disastrous shooting at the Bustamante place. They had hauled the surviving Bustamantes to jail and a doctor, and Albert Stout's body home to his family. They had had enough of chasing a bad-man.

The fugitive seemed to have an angel riding on his shoulder. He had worked his way through a dozen tight posse nets. Times, men were sure they had seen him, but when they got to the place, he was always gone. Perhaps he had never been there at all.

Kelly watched firelight falling across Joe Florey's face. The old man had changed during these long hard days, and not for the better. "You tired, Joe?"

"Have I complained?"

"No, I'm thinkin' maybe you ought to."

"If you're tired, you can always turn around and go home. Next posse comes along I can get somebody else to side me."

Kelly shook his head. "I'm doin' all right if you are."

"I'm fine. This trip has made me twenty years younger."

That was a damn lie, Kelly thought. Twenty years *older*, maybe. Times he had been afraid Joe would fall from the saddle in total exhaustion. But there was a leather tough-ness in the old man that always came to the surface like a second wind and made him last until darkness forced them to stop.

He must sure have been something when he was young,
Kelly thought with admiration. *I wish I could have seen him.*

Joe said, "I been thinkin' about that little girl of yours,
Kelly. She could've had that baby by now."

Kelly nodded soberly. "I know."

"Don't you want to go back and see?"

"Hell, yes, I want to go back. But I told her I would stay
out till this was over, one way or the other. She knows
where I'm at. I've sent her a message every day by one officer or another."

"But you ain't been able to hear anything from her."

"I'll hear it all . . . when we get back to Domingo."

Kelly squinted at the figures moving across the brushy
flat, seeming to float in the heat waves. "Somebody's
comin', Joe. Looks like a man on horseback, leadin' a horse
at the end of a rope." Joe Florey had been concentrating
on horse tracks. He looked up, pulling his hat brim down
lower to shade his weary eyes. He grunted. "We ain't
passed two hours, hardly, that somebody ain't come to see
who we are and what we're up to. All them reports about
people seein' Fernandez . . . I think most of the time they
been seein' us. I swear, I don't see how that Mexican keeps
gettin' by."

"Luck," said Kelly.

"Luck hell!" Joe snorted. "He's one smart boy . . . must
have an eye like an eagle." Joe dismounted, his old legs stiff
and sore. Painfully he knelt, fingering the tracks. "These
ain't hardly blowed out around the edges yet. We been
catchin' up to him a right smart." He pointed. "That
Mexican got off here and walked around a little bit.
Relieved his kidneys, and I think he knelt down, too. I see
what looks to me like a knee print."

"Prayin', maybe.

"I got a notion he was checkin' the mare's feet. He's
been movin' awful slow. I've had a hunch for a good while
that she's goin' lame on him."

"He's put a lot of miles on her."

127

"And on us, too." Florey was beginning to show a little excitement, as much as he was ever likely to. "If them other hombres don't stumble onto him first, I'd say we stand a good chance of catchin' up to him. Even a turtle can go a long ways if he keeps at it long enough."

Kelly squinted again at the oncoming horseman. The rider did not hold his interest long, however. The sorrel mare he was leading took Kelly's eye. She was favoring her right hind foot.

He had seen the sorrel mare only once, the day Chacho Fernandez had ridden her up to the front of Griffin Holliday's house. Nevertheless, he was almost sure this was the same mare.

The rider, a young cowboy, pulled to a stop. "You-all'd be followin' the Mexican's tracks, I expect?"

"We was," Joe replied testily, "till you come along and messed them up. What's that mare you got?"

"It's *his!*" the cowboy said eagerly. "I found her down yonder a ways. He'd turned her a-loose."

Kelly and Joe Florey gave each other a long glance. Florey bent for a close look at the mare's feet and at the tracks she made. "She's the one, all right. By God, I told you she was lame!"

No wonder they used to say Joe could trail the west wind across flat rock! Kelly said. "He's caught him a fresh one, finally. He'll be movin' faster now."

The cowboy shook his head. "Not unless he's ridin bareback. I found his saddle."

Kelly caught a sharp breath. "She doesn't look that lame. Looks like he'd've ridden her at least till he got him another, no matter how bad she was."

Joe looked thoughtfully at the mare. "Maybe he just loves horses."

"And hates sheriffs." Kelly turned back to the cowboy. "Tie her up and take us to where you found the saddle. No use for us to poke along here if you already know where the tracks go."

They loped to make time. In a little while the cowboy

drew rein and pointed. "Right over yonder is where I found her. She was grazin' along by herself. I taken a look at her brand and markin's, and I remembered the description they gave out. I was takin' her up to ranch headquarters to get on the telephone when I come across you-all."

Joe Florey was impatient to see where the cowboy had found the saddle, because it was from there that Fernandez' trail would start fresh again. The cowboy had made a lot of boot tracks stomping around the site. That angered Joe, but it was no real handicap. He moved south a hundred feet and started cutting back and forth. Shortly he came up with boot prints.

Kelly felt a glow of satisfaction. "Afoot. It ought to go easier from now on."

Joe Florey disagreed. "He'll move slower, but that ain't necessarily in our favor. A man on foot can hide his tracks a lot easier than a man on horseback. He's just got two feet to cover for."

The cowboy said, "I'll be glad to come along and help you."

Kelly declined the offer but gave his thanks. "It would be more help if you would go on back to the ranch, like you were sayin', and send word out for everybody to be watchin' for a man on foot. And see if you can get somebody to catch up to us with a pair of fresh horses we can have the borrow of."

"And some grub," Joe Florey added. "We ain't been richly fed the last few days."

"I'll sure do it," the cowboy declared eagerly. "And if anybody ever asks you who it was that found the mare, tell them it was Artis Paxton."

"We'll tell them," Kelly promised. He watched as the cowboy rode away. Artis Paxton was a young man now, in his early twenties. Someday he would tell his grandchildren that he was the one who found the mare that carried Chacho Fernandez five days on the greatest manhunt in Texas.

The cowboy thought of something and came riding back in a lope. "Hey! Reckon who owns the mare now?"

Joe Florey grumbled about people asking fool questions. Kelly had to admit he had never given the subject a minute's thought. "I suppose that'll be for a court to decide."

"I'm puttin' in a claim on her," the cowboy said. "I want you-all as my witnesses that I was the one found her. She could be worth some money . . . the mare that carried the sheriff-killer."

"We'll remember you," Kelly promised. "Ardis Paxton."

"Artis," the cowboy corrected him. "That's with a T."

"With a T," Kelly said. "I'll write it down. You see about gettin' us some fresh horses now, you hear? I doubt we'll be movin' very fast."

Presently Joe reined up and motioned for Kelly to stay back. The old man dismounted stiffly, studying the ground while he steadied his legs, then knelt for a closer look. "I'll be damned!" he said, half under his breath. "I wisht you'd looky here."

Kelly looked, but he was not sure what he saw. He could see an impression left by a man lying in the sand behind a mesquite, but that didn't mean much to him. What was unusual about a man stopping to rest himself?

"Right yonder," Joe pointed, "not ten feet away, is a set of horse tracks. That cowboy Paxton, he's the one that left them. He rode through here before he come upon that mare. The Mexican was layin' here hidin'. That cowboy rode by so close, that Mexican could've spit on him."

Kelly shrugged. "You can't blame the kid. He's a cowboy, not a peace officer."

"That ain't the point. The point is, why didn't that Mexican shoot him and take his horse? It'd've been like takin' candy away from a baby."

Kelly shrugged again. "Who knows why a Mexican does anything?"

"If he was a killer like everybody says, that's just what he'd've done. He'd have him a horse, and he wouldn't have to worry about that kid runnin' for help."

"Maybe he was afraid somebody would hear the shot."

Joe looked at Kelly and shook his head. "You just don't

see it, do you, Kelly? The way you couldn't see me stayin'
on the force. You looked so hard at one or two of my little
faults that you couldn't see how many good points I still
had."

"Griffin Holliday is in his grave. You sayin' that's a little
thing?"

Joe Florey seemed about to argue, then gave it up and
turned away, muttering. "And they claim I'm the one that
don't see good any more."

TWELVE

Chacho Fernandez had never had occasion to reflect on the fact that a man can see much less from afoot than from the back of a horse. It was surprising, now that he was confronted by the proposition in a situation where it truly counted, that a few feet less of height could make such a drastic difference.

On the other hand, if it was more difficult to see, it was also difficult to be seen. He wondered if it would have been so easy to have eluded that cowboy's notice three days ago if he had still been riding the sorrel mare. As it was, he had come within a breath of stepping out into the open, unaware that anyone was so near to him. He had seen the rider just in time to duck back behind the foliage, and to drop on his belly behind the heavy trunk of an old granddaddy mesquite where last year's cured grass had grown up thick and tall, and the new spring growth within it was green with life.

For a moment Chacho was afraid the cowboy would ride

right over him. Chacho had drawn the pistol from his waistband, and he had considered how simple it would be to get himself a horse again. The temptation had been almost overpowering. One more gringo gone from this earth . . . where would be the loss? There were already so many. . . . And if they caught him they would hang or shoot him anyway for the killing of the sheriff. Could they kill him twice because he had added some stupid cowboy to the list?

Chacho had leveled the pistol and steadied it on the mesquite trunk, sighting on the cowboy through the thick grass. At this distance he could not miss. The only risk was that the horse would panic at the shot and run away before Chacho could leap up and catch him. Or that someone within hearing would come to investigate the shot. But given a fresh horse, Chacho knew he would have better than an even chance to get away. He had had possemen ride close to him many times in the last few days, and none had ever seen him so far as he knew, much less caught him.

He sighted across the barrel at the cowboy's chest. But he made the mistake of lifting his gaze to the fresh young face, of seeing the carefree eyes of youth, of hearing the tuneless little ditty the cowboy whistled.

It brought back to him the sight of blood in the ranch yard, the horror of seeing his brother and the sheriff dead. A chill ran through him, and his hands trembled. He tried to squeeze the trigger but found no strength for it. He looked at the happy young face and saw the dying sheriff.

Shoot him! cried an angry inner voice, but Chacho could not. He lay there, the pistol still extended, and watched the cowboy ride by so close that Chacho fancied he could feel the warmth of his breath.

Then the cowboy was past him and riding on. Chacho turned over onto his right elbow and looked, trembling from the stress. *How could he have missed seeing me when I could see him so plainly?*

Fool! the inner voice blistered him. *I could have used that horse. I did not have to shoot him if I did not want to; I could have taken the horse away and left that cowboy here afoot, as I am afoot now. I could still do it. I could run up from behind and catch him.*

But he lay there, not moving until the cowboy was well gone. As calm gradually returned, he still regretted not getting the horse, but he was glad he had not shot the cowboy. Not in all the nights since the shooting had he ever slept deeply and well. At some time every night he would wake up in a cold sweat, shouting at the sheriff that he had not wanted to kill him.

If one dead man could be such a cross for a man to bear, might two not drive him to his grave?

God, it was a terrible thing to have a dead man for a companion all this time!

He had been afoot three days now, moving much slower than he had done on horseback, sure he was putting in more miles than before because he could not see the trails so clearly, because he did not feel safe in crossing the open places and went out of his way to stay in the brush.

The modest amount of food he had brought from the Bustamante place had long since run out. He had abandoned the bridle because the longer he carried it the heavier it seemed to be. When at last he dropped it into a bush, it was as if he had shed fifty pounds. He hung onto the rope awhile longer, knowing that without a rope he stood little chance of catching a loose horse. But eventually even the rope became a burden, and he hid it in a rat's nest.

By now he had given up any hope of finding, much less catching, a loose horse out in these big open pastures he was crossing. If he managed to steal a horse he would have to catch it in some rancher's pen, perhaps a night horse kept up for gathering the remuda in the early morning.

But to do this he would have to approach a ranch headquarters, and he had not mustered the nerve. He had seen few on this long journey, and those few simply seemed to have too many people around them. The risk of discovery seemed much greater than the risk in going on the way he was.

Late the day after he had turned the mare loose, he came upon a lonely little house all by itself in the middle of one of those big brushy regions that seemed so common as a man moved nearer to Mexico. He had lain up in the protection of some dead brush and studied it a long time, trying to assess the risk in going down there. He knew within reason that it was a Mexican place, rather than Anglo. It had that dirt-poor look about it.

That judgment was vindicated when a man and a couple of boys came in at dusk, leading a tired old mule with the harness still on it. Somewhere, out of Chacho's sight, must be a field of some sort, probably corn. If it were later in the season he could borrow some corn ears and fill the aching void of his stomach, but this was too early.

He watched the man and one of the boys unharness the mule and turn it loose while another boy walked to a small pen. Chacho heard the squealing of pigs, fighting for a share as the boy fed them.

Young suckling pigs, some of them, judging by the noise.

Darkness came, and the Mexican family went into the house. There appeared to be no woman. A widower and two young sons, Chacho figured. This was hard country on a woman; the mortality rate was high. He smelled woodsmoke as the people began fixing their supper. It brought the hunger pain back with a jolting violence.

Maybe if I went down there and told them I was hungry they would feed me. But they would ask questions. They would want to know why I am out here alone and afoot. Even if I did not tell them they would probably guess. Surely they know about me. The officers probably come by here every day, looking for me. Surely there is a reward. A family as poor as this could not help but think of the reward.

Diego Bustamante's warning kept coming back to him. *Trust no one.*

In full darkness he crept down to the barn. He looked at the old mule, which had finished its ration of corn and stood listless and hipshot in the brush corral. It would be nice to substitute four feet for his own two. But he hated to rob this poor family, which as far as he could tell had only this one mule. He had not seen so much even as a milk cow, though he had heard a goat bleating out in the brush.

Anyway, the mule was old and probably slow. Of what use would it be if a posse saw him and gave chase? A spotted goat could probably give the mule thirty yards and outrun him from here to the field. The mule would likely cause Chacho to be seen, and if he were seen he would surely be run down.

He passed on by the mule and came to the pigpen. He could see some good-sized shoats, milk-fat. There, at least, was a temporary answer to his hunger. He slipped over the fence, grabbed one of the shoats by its hind legs and climbed out again. The pig squealed shrilly. The old sow, suddenly awakened from lethargy, raised a commotion. She sent her other pigs scattering in confusion, all squealing and adding to the din. Several dogs came rushing out from under the poor frame house, barking and raising hell.

Chacho cursed under his breath. He had to stop this pig's squealing and kicking. Throwing it to the ground and holding its struggling body beneath his knee, he fished a knife from his pocket and slit the pig's throat. With all this racket around him, and with that man and his sons bound to come out carrying a gun — provided they had one — he could not stay here to bleed the pig properly. He picked up the struggling, kicking pig and broke into a run, blood streaming behind him. The dogs gave chase, and he could hear a man shouting somewhere back in the darkness.

When he had gained some distance he stopped and confronted the pursuing dogs. He laid down the dying pig and picked up a heavy stick. He fetched a couple of the dogs a sound lick across the nose. They finally retreated, barking but giving him room. When he had made perhaps half a mile, the dogs turned back and went home.

Chacho stopped and gutted the pig so it would not spoil, but he did not want to build a fire that would give him away in the darkness. He walked through the rest of

137

the night, putting all the miles he could between himself and that house. At daylight he dug a hole in the sand, gathered dry wood, carefully built a fire with one of his jealously hoarded matches, and set half of the pig in to barbeque. He could not wait for it to be completely done. He began cutting chunks off of it almost as soon as the blood stopped dripping. He carried the other half with him, cooking it late the same day and finishing it. He felt stronger than he had in days.

Now it was coming on to the end of the third full day since he had given up the mare, and two days since he had eaten the pig. He was weak again from hunger. His boots were worn so thin that he could feel the heat of the noonday sand through the soles almost as strongly as if his feet had been bare. Times his vision played tricks on him. When this condition came upon him he was compelled to seek a hiding place and rest, for if a posse were to come along he might not see it until too late. He would siesta uneasily, closing his eyes but trying never to shut out all the sounds. More than once he heard horsemen passing near. He had not the slightest doubt they were looking for him.

Damn them, won't they ever quit? I have had time to have gotten across the river by now, if my luck had been good. Why don't they decide that is what I have done and give up the chase?

Afoot and staying always within easy reach of protecting brush, he had been forced to stray from the trails he had known when he was running horses to the border. But he thought he was still on the general track, and he was sure that not far down here he would come upon a little Mexican village known as Hermoso. *Hermoso* meant handsome, and that used to bring a grin to Chacho's face every time he saw the place. The only thing he had ever seen handsome about it was the fact that it had a couple of good roads leading out.

But he thought it might look better to him now. A town meant people, and food, and perhaps even a horse. He kept walking in the direction he thought would take him there, and finally he came upon a road he thought he knew. He did not cross it because he did not want to leave tracks that could be seen, but he paralleled it, staying back a respectable distance. About sundown he came in sight of it and stopped, lying on his stomach and staring at the town through the shielding grass.

He had a long time to study it before darkness came. He memorized every house he could see. He had time to study the people who came and went. He saw no Anglo face, only Mexicans. Normally he would have considered that to be good, but now it made no real difference. There were too many who might betray him for reward. He had to assume that he had no friends anywhere north of the river, none at least but Julio Carrasco. Carrasco could be trusted, Esteban had said.

By dark Chacho had picked his house. He did not want to go where many people dwelled, for surely he would awaken someone. He picked an adobe house where he had seen no one enter or leave except a woman, a young woman if his eyesight was to be trusted at the distance. He had not seen a child; if there was one, it was probably small. If there was a man, he was working away from here and had not come home.

He had also spotted a corral where four or five horses had been fed hay, meaning they would probably be kept up for the night.

The woman's house first, then, for food, once she had had time to go to sleep. Then the corral, where he could pick himself the best-looking horse. Then, *adiós, por alla.*

At dark he moved up. He had no intention of going into the house until he felt the woman was asleep. With luck, he could take some food and never awaken her. But he wanted to be sure no one else entered the place unbeknown to him; there were surprises enough in this world without carelessly leaving the door open for them. He found an old shed where he could sit in the comfortable darkness and observe the house without being seen. There was even a bench on which he could stretch his tired body. He had to be careful he did not drop off to sleep. It would be a hell of a thing to wake up and find it daylight.

He watched the lamplight through the open window and listened to the quiet passage of a little foot and horse traffic down the single crooked dirt street. He saw the lamp wink out, as others were doing all over the village. He felt a prickling of impatience, but he knew a woman did not go to sleep immediately simply because she had put her light out. He had to give her time.

He gave her what he judged to be an hour. By now he heard no noise except the picking of a guitar, far up the street, and the crying of a baby several houses away. He thought of that cantina, and how fine it would be to step in there and order himself enough beer to drown a dog, or enough *pulque* to choke a full-grown mule.

He got up from the bench, moved cautiously to the door, and flattened himself against the wall, in the shadows, listening carefully. He heard nothing. He carefully pushed against the door and found that it opened easily. He opened it only a little at first, listening again. He thought he heard the even breathing of a person asleep. He pushed a little more and stepped inside.

He quickly made out the general pattern of the single room. It was bedroom, kitchen, and all. The woman slept in a near corner, almost against the door. It was a double bed, but no one shared it with her.

Ah, he thought, *poor woman, what a waste for her.*

He made out the shape of a small iron stove, the kind the gringos had introduced into this part of the country and which had become common in many Mexican homes. Beyond that was a wooden chest he knew had to be a pantry.

Tiptoeing across the room, he found a pan of cold bread on the back of the stove. He could not control himself. He grabbed bread with both hands and shoved it into his mouth, swallowing before it was half chewed. He almost choked. He did not want to eat it all here. He wanted to save some. That, and whatever else he could find, might have to see him all the way to Carrasco's.

Carefully he opened the wooden chest. He had to feel as much as see what was in it. He found a little sack that he knew was potatoes. He found a sack of shelled corn, ready to be ground for tortillas or whatever. He wished for meat but saw no sign of any. Perhaps the woman had a small shed of some kind out in back where meat might hang from a rafter, out of reach of the dogs. But a woman alone like this might not be able to afford meat at all. Well, a man could make do on corn and potatoes. He had seen times he had done worse.

It was on his conscience that he had to steal from a woman, especially a poor woman of his own people. A fleeting thought came that someday he would find a way to repay her. But he knew that was an idle hope. He could never come back here.

He heard a metallic click behind him and froze. He knew instantly what it was, and the hair seemed to rise on his neck.

A woman's voice said, "Raise your hands. Slowly. I have the pistol cocked, and I know how to fire it."

Chacho was too surprised to do anything except obey. He let the sack of corn drop to the floor as he lifted both hands over his head.

Damn the luck! To be caught by a woman!

He was sure she was not bluffing about that pistol. There was no mistaking the sound of the hammer going back. Maybe she could shoot straight and maybe she couldn't. He did not care to find out.

"Careful," he said. "I did not mean you any harm. Careful with that pistol or you will do *me* very great harm."

He turned slowly, trying not to scare her any worse than she already was. A frightened woman with a cocked and loaded pistol in her hands was an exceedingly dangerous thing.

He saw that she was sitting straight up in bed, a huge old pistol in both hands at full arm's length, pointed directly at him. If she fired it, the recoil would carry it straight back over her head. But he probably would not live to see the surprise in her face.

"Careful with that thing," he said again, more nervously now. "If you fire it, it may do us both much harm." *Me more than you, of course,* he thought.

The woman never wavered. She began calling out for help. "Mauricio! Rosendo! Come help me! Bring a gun!"

Uselessly Chacho pleaded, "I have come to do you no harm. I only need a little food and I will be on my way. There is no need to bother these other people."

But the other people already were bothered. They began coming in, most of them in their underwear or other night-clothes, a couple bringing guns. Chacho swallowed hard as they lighted the lamp and stared at him. He counted three guns pointed at him, including the woman's. She never lowered it.

Despair came, and his shoulders slumped.

I am dead, he told himself. All the pent-up fear and anger and helplessness of the long flight seemed to fall upon him like a ton of stones, and he sank to his knees, unable to stop the trembling. *I am dead. It is better I do something now to make them shoot me, better than facing those gringos with their ropes. They are an exceedingly cruel people, those gringos. They are not truly human.*

The woman was crying now that the danger was past. *Why were women forever crying?* Chacho wondered. "Who is he?" half a dozen wanted to know, but the woman had no answer. He was a stranger to her.

Then a middle-aged man in a long nightshirt stepped closer. He picked up the lamp and extended it toward Chacho's face. "My God!" he said finally, "I know this man. He has been in my store." He spoke directly to Chacho. "You are the one the gringos all seek. You are Chacho Fernandez."

Chacho saw no gain in denying it. He nodded dismally, knowing he had no chance. His throat tightened, and he fought back the awful fear that struggled to break free. He could already feel the gringo rope burning his neck, strangling him.

He heard the people murmur with surprise and awe.

Chacho! Chacho Fernandez! Is it really he? Is it truly the one who killed all the *rinches*, all those sheriffs? Yes, it is he, the one the people are all telling of, the brave Chacho who laughs at the gringos and kills all their sheriffs.

But he does not look like the one we have heard about. He is an ordinary man, not tall at all, not big. And his clothes. Look at those rags. Is that the way a *rinche-killer* would look?

He is trembling, too, as if he were afraid. But surely the Chacho would never tremble. He would never be afraid of anything, for he has been heard to laugh in the face of death. He has been seen to ride into a hundred *rinches*, firing his guns and laughing in their faces as they fell from their saddles and died in the dung of their own horses.

Perhaps he does not tremble from fear. If he was taking food, he was hungry. Does a man's body not tremble when the hunger weakens him? Go, some of you. Go bring him food. Bring him meat, good meat. Bring him frijoles to fill out his ribs. Bring him tequila, the best tequila.

Maria, he is the size of your good Ricardo who died last fall. He needs something to replace these rags, and your husband would be proud to know that the great Chacho wears his clothes. Find something for him, Maria. Find something worthy for a man who has done what all of us wanted to do. Nothing shoddy. The best for him, only the best.

Chacho blinked, unbelieving. This was a dream, a wild dream. He had expected death at the hands of these people. Instead, they gave him adulation. They stared at him as if he were a saint come down to bless them and assure them their place in Heaven.

These things they were saying — not one of them was true. Where did they hear such things? What preposterous stories were being told?

He tried to tell them, but they would not listen. Suddenly they were all gathered around him, slapping him on the back, pushing him into a chair at the table, bringing him food and drink, ten times more than he could possibly find room for. They were telling him that all over Mexican Texas, people were lighting candles for him in the churches, praying he would be safe from all those officers, praying he would find the strength to lead them up and out of the gringo domination, to lead them in reclaiming all that stolen land from the Nueces River to the Rio Grande, to bring it back into Mexico where it belonged.

Chacho gave up arguing. They would hear only what they chose to hear, and the truth was the least of this. One would almost think they had been listening to the fanatic ramblings of Esteban Bustamante.

They sacked up more food than he thought he could carry. The woman Maria wanted him to take her husband's good suit, but Chacho chose working clothes he thought would serve him better. He exchanged his worn-out boots for a pair that had been worn only to church.

And last, they brought him a horse. He had intended to steal one, but when they gathered and so willingly gave him one, he came near crying. They offered to send someone to show him the best way to the river, but he did not want to endanger anyone needlessly. He assured them he knew the way; he could travel better alone.

When he left they were all standing there to bid him goodbye . . . men, women, children, even the village priest. Chacho was still a little stunned.

This could not be real, any of it. What did they think he was? He had not asked for any of this adulation, this great false reputation that somehow had fallen upon his shoulders.

All he had wanted was what was his, one sorrel mare he had rightfully earned.

He did not want to stir a rebellion.

He did not want to become some kind of a god.

What in Heaven's name did they think he was?

THIRTEEN

Domingo attorney Baltazar Fierro had been to the jail
every day to visit old Esteban Bustamante. The
wounded *viejo*, the fiery revolutionary, lay on a cot in
a cell behind a set of iron bars three Percheron horses could not have bent. He was charged with the
murder of Albert Stout, although it was common knowledge that Stout had been shot accidentally by one of his fellow possemen. Somebody had to shoulder the blame, and
Esteban was willing.

In those gradually shortening periods when his strength
was up he would rail at his jailers, protesting a hundred
injustices imposed upon his people by the damnable gringos, proclaiming that he had indeed killed the one named
Stout, and that he had killed many more that night besides.
Those lying gringos had carried away the others in secrecy
to rob him of the honor due him for sending them all to
hell.

He wanted them to shoot him for killing Stout. It was an

honorable way for a warrior to die. But the gringos would not have to shoot him. Day by day, Fierro could see the old man sinking. He had suffered worse wounds in his time, but he had been younger and stronger then, like his grandson Anselmo who was beginning to mend now. A few more days and Esteban would be gone. He would die in bed in this dim gray cell, the shadow of those window-bars lying across his face.

Fierro knew Esteban had killed nobody that night, but it was a needless thing to argue about. Let the old man have his honor, and let the gringos have their culprit. This way everybody was served . . . everybody but truth, and truth was never expected to have much of a show.

The old man's voice was weak, but there was still an eagerness about it. "Friend Fierro, what is the news today of Chacho?"

Fierro looked around to see if the jailer was within hearing. One could never trust these *gueros*. They all pretended not to understand Spanish, but often as not they knew far more than they let on. It was a typical trick of theirs to gain an advantage. "Some of the gringo newspapers are saying the search is hopeless. They are saying that by this time he has surely gotten across the river and is safe in Mexico."

"They will not get him, not that Chacho."

"But he is not yet in Mexico, old friend. I have gotten word just now through some friends that the night before last he was in Hermoso. The people there fed him and gave him a horse and sent him on his way."

"Hermoso!" The old man groaned. "That is a long way from the river."

"Many of the searchers have given up, sure he is in Mexico. Many of the gringos who went out from this place are home again, saying he escaped."

"What of that deputy, that Willcox?"

"He is still down there somewhere. He wants to become the new sheriff. He would bring Chacho's head home in a sack if he could."

"That Willcox!" The old man cursed vigorously. "I should have killed him along with all those others!"

Fierro motioned with his hands. "Lie still, old friend. You do yourself harm when you rise up that way. Lie still. Chacho is too watchful to let himself be caught by one like that Willcox. But there is another I am much more worried about, the old man Florey. They say he can trail anything. They say he has been behind Chacho like a bloodhound, always pressing him. One like that Willcox makes much noise and talks of great things and does nothing. But a quiet one like that Florey is dangerous. He comes up from behind when a man is not looking. That, I think, is Chacho's great danger."

"Chacho could do what we used to do in the old days, circle back on his own trail and set an ambush."

"Perhaps. But I do not think that is in his nature. He is not an old revolutionary like you."

Esteban stared at the plastered ceiling in thoughtful silence. "I confess, Fierro, I have been a little disappointed in Chacho. It was long in my mind that he was a man who could fire our people into a new revolution and throw off this damned gringo yoke. But he never had an instinct for the kill."

Fierro nodded dolefully. "Yes, it is a pity, for I think he is one the people would have followed if he had chosen to lead. You should hear what is being said about him. Did you know they are already singing *corridos* about him, telling stories about things that never happened? The people are excited about him as they have been excited about no one man that I can remember. If he were to say, 'Rise up,' I believe they would rise up. If he were to say, 'We go to war,' they would come running to join him."

The attorney rubbed his hand over his eyes. "I have had a wild thought, Esteban, a bad thought that shames me. But it keeps coming back. I have found myself almost wishing they would catch Chacho, that they would kill him."

The old man flared. "Fierro. You should burn out your tongue!"

"I know. I wish the thought had never come to me, but now it keeps coming back. I keep thinking that if he were

147

to die at gringo hands the people would be so enraged that they would rise up and fight. I keep thinking that in death he might do what he will never do alive . . . he could lead our people to fight their way back to freedom."

The old man did not reply. He lay staring up at the ceiling. Fierro looked at him with a growing concern. "Esteban. Esteban! Are you all right?"

Esteban finally took notice of his friend's anxiety. "All this talk has made me tired. Suddenly I do not feel like talking any more."

Fierro stood up, remorseful. "I should never have burdened you with my foolish thoughts. I am sorry, old friend. You rest now, and I will see you again tomorrow."

"Tomorrow," said Esteban, not looking at him. He continued to stare at the ceiling a long time after Fierro had gone. His lips moved in silence as he posed arguments to himself and as he answered those arguments. Anger would flare in his face, and it would subside. Times, the silent words on his lips would come alive in angry sounds, and once they brought the jailer to see what that damn crazy old Mexican was raving about this time.

Finally Esteban put aside his doubts and called to the jailer. When the man did not come immediately, Esteban began to shout speculation about his ancestry, about his manhood. The jailer pushed through the outer iron door and strode angrily down the short aisle between the cells.

"Old man, you shut your mouth or I'll tie a gag on you."

The words were English and meant nothing to Esteban. Even in Spanish he would not have paid attention to them. The old man said, "You understand me when I speak Spanish; I know you do, so do not pretend otherwise. I have something important to say."

The jailer stared at him contemptuously. "All right, say it. Then I will gag you."

"The deputy Willcox . . . do you know where he is right now?"

"Maybe I do."

"Could you ring that gringo telephone you have and reach him?"

The deputy began to take a little interest. "I could get someone who could find him."

"Then do so. Tell him I know where he can catch Chacho Fernandez."

It had not taken the messenger long to locate Odom Willcox and get him to the sheriff's office in the courthouse far south of Domingo. Willcox had been around the area several days, jumping at every rumor, riding horses to the point of exhaustion and limping in frustrated. He had made it a point that everyone should know he was the man who had served directly under Griffin Holliday, and that he was the one who intended personally to dispatch that murdering Mexican son of a bitch and carry him home like a sheep-killing wolf, tied dead across a packhorse. Chacho Fernandez might get by everybody else, but to cross that river he was going to have to walk over Odom Willcox's dead body, and they hadn't raised a Mexican yet who was man enough to do that.

Willcox rang up Central on the local sheriff's wall telephone and told her to connect him with the sheriff's office in Domingo. He hung up then and began pacing the floor, smoking cigarettes and waiting for her to call him back.

He didn't like this office. This county even had a Mexican sheriff. Hell of a note, the way he saw it. Damn people down here thought they were as good as white. They wouldn't get away with a thing like that up in Domingo, not for a minute. He stared contemptuously at the deputy who had gone to fetch him. He was Anglo, but that didn't mean much as far as Willcox was concerned. What kind of a white man was it that would work for a Mexican? Couldn't be much to him.

Willcox was worried about that telephone call. He had been afraid the county judge and the commissioners court might have decided to call him home and cut off the expense to the county of having him roaming around down here when there were any number of state officers doing that without cost to the local taxpayers.

Goddamn them, he thought anxiously, *they wouldn't do that!* Surely they wouldn't do that, and rob him of his chance to get that Mexican himself.

Well, by God, he wouldn't let them do it. No sir! He smacked his fist into the palm of his left hand, startling the local deputy, who had gone back to some paperwork at his rolltop desk. No, sir, he would pay his own expenses if they were so goddamned tight. They weren't going to rob him of this chance to show he was as good a man as Griffin Holliday, and that he could do the job.

Hell, he was a *better* man than Griffin Holliday. Griff had fooled around and let a damn Mexican kill him. No Mexican would ever get the chance to kill Odom Willcox.

I'll shoot the son of a bitch first and then ask questions later. High time them damn people know who the boss is, anyway!

The telephone rang, and he grabbed it before the deputy could get up from his desk to answer it. He shouted into the mouthpiece. A man had to shout at these things or nobody could hear him. Then he listened, and as he listened his eyes widened.

"You sure?" he shouted into the telephone. "That old man could be lyin'. They'd all rather lie to you than tell you the truth." He listened awhile longer and finally said, "All right, Sid. If the old man is lyin' I'll take care of him when I get back. If he ain't, I'll bring home Chacho Fernandez . . . dead!"

He put the receiver on the wishbone hook and gave the crank half a turn so Central would know she could disconnect. He turned back to the deputy, who was watching him with considerable interest.

"You tell me how to find a place that belongs to a man named Carrasco. Julio Carrasco."

Four hours later and far west of town, Willcox sat on his horse and looked down on a small rock house at the edge of a clearing in the low brush. "*Looks* like a horsethief outfit, even. An hour's good ride south and they're at the Rio

Grande. Plenty of brush cover all the way. Slick, these people. But not slick enough."

He motioned to the three men who had moved their horses up beside him and rode to surround the house. Three dogs trotted out, barking furiously. Smoke curled up from the chimney. Willcox brought his rifle up to cradle it in his arms and stopped his horse in front of the door.

"Carrasco! Julio Carrasco!"

"*Quién es?*" came a voice from inside.

"Never mind who it is. We've got this house surrounded. You step on out here where we can see you!"

The wooden door swung inward. A Mexican man stood there with a sack tied around his waist, his hands white with flour.

"You Julio Carrasco?" Willcox demanded.

The man nodded apprehensively, looking at all the rifles pointed at him. "Yes, that is my name."

"You know a man named Chacho Fernandez?"

"No," said Carrasco, "I know no such man."

Willcox squeezed the trigger. Carrasco slammed back against the half-open door, clutching for something to hold to. Willcox said, "I hate a liar" and shot him again. He caught his companions by surprise. He demanded, "You-all seen him go for his gun, didn't you?"

The dogs were in a frenzy. Willcox gave a curt nod toward one which was nipping at his horse's heels. "Shoot him! Shoot them all!"

The dogs were dispatched in a sudden volley.

Willcox swung to the ground. "All right, boys, let's find a place to hide the horses. No tellin' how long a wait it'll be."

151

The town of Hermoso proved to be the worst snag Joe Florey and Kelly Sadler had struck in many days. It was made up of people who all seemed to be deaf and dumb. The dogs talked about as much as the people did and seemed far less hostile. These villagers had never even heard of Chacho Fernandez, so far as Kelly could find out. Yet the tracks plainly showed that he had walked in here, probably sometime last night. The secretive manner of the people was proof enough to Kelly that they did indeed know much, and that they meant to tell none of it.

While Kelly tried fruitlessly to find out something by questioning the people, Joe Florey was south of town trying to cut a trail. He had come to know Chacho's footprints as well as if they had been a signature written on a legal document. He found them nowhere.

He came back after more than an hour. "I think he either stole a horse here or these people gave him one."

Kelly had seen several horses scattered around town, not to mention a number of mules. The opportunity had certainly been here. If Chacho had stolen a horse, someone would be angry enough to talk, like that farmer who had lost a good young pig the other night.

No, he thought with growing impatience, these people had given Chacho a horse. But what horse? What kind of tracks did the horse make?

Joe Florey made a fresh start, looking now for horse tracks instead of bootprints. There were many; a lot of the people who lived here tended fields south of town, or tended stock running loose. How to choose from among so many kinds of tracks was a riddle beyond Kelly's capability. Joe Florey did not seem to be in despair. He worked gradually south, eliminating one set of tracks from consideration because it veered off toward a field, another because it led toward a herd of goats scattered to the west.

"My feelin'," he said, "is that Fernandez left here in the night. He probably used the stars for a guide because he wouldn't want to use the main trail. I think the tracks that lead straightest south are likely to be his."

Finally, a long way south of Hermoso, Joe Florey had settled upon one set. "If I'm wrong," he conceded, "we're blowed plumb up. But all the other tracks we've followed so far have led off somewhere or turned back. These are the only ones that've kept right on goin'. If we can ever catch up to the horse that made them, we'll find Chacho Fernandez on his back."

FOURTEEN

Chacho liked the horse they had given him in Hermoso. It was a black gelding with one stocking foot and a white blaze on its face. Its gait was rougher than the sorrel mare's, and it had a tendency to be a little cold-jawed, to respond rather slowly to the bit. But Chacho judged the animal ought to be strong of wind, should go a long way without letting him down. With any kind of luck, and a rest or two along the way, this black should get him all the way to Carrasco's, and then on down to the river. He wondered idly if the horse was much of a swimmer. Raised in this desert-type country, it had probably never been in water past its belly.

Well, swimming was a thing that came naturally to most animals, he supposed. He had delivered a number of horses down to Carrasco in the time he was pursuing that trade, and he had never heard of one drowning while crossing the Rio Grande.

This horse had one advantage over the sorrel mare. Its

153

black color would be harder for the *rinches* to see. A black was nigh perfect for a man riding the brush country, on the dodge; it blended in.

For the twentieth time he fingered the almost-new shirt the woman Maria had given him, and he looked down at the good boots shoved to the heels into the *tapaderos*, the covered stirrups of the Mexico saddle. He dug a tortilla out of the sack and ate it dry as he rode.

It still bothered him, the way those people had received him. He had expected hostility. Anytime a Mexican did something which drastically displeased the Anglo authorities, other Mexicans paid for it in a dozen ways, some subtle and some blunt. Something dreadful had been visited upon the Bustamantes as a result of his killing that sheriff. A man who brings such misfortune upon his people has no right to expect their gratitude.

And there was the matter of the reward. Surely there were some in Hermoso who would like to have turned him in for whatever rewards were being offered on his head. Even when they were feeding him so generously and bringing him clothing and a horse, he had harbored a nagging suspicion that they were simply delaying him until the *rinches* could get there. In the end he had decided they meant all these things they were saying to him. They might have lied with their words, but they could not have lied to him with their eyes.

They had made a hero of him, and he had no wish to be one. What had he done to earn this? He had killed a sheriff, that was all. It was nothing for a man to be proud of unless the man were a fanatic like old Esteban. It was a thing for shame, not for pride.

What was the matter with these people that they could not see it?

Well, soon it would not matter what they thought. Soon — perhaps tomorrow — he would be at Carrasco's, and Carrasco would see him safely across the river.

He heard a commotion somewhere ahead of him in the brush, and he jerked on the reins, pulling the black up short. Instinctively he leaned down over the horse's neck to make a low silhouette. His impulse was to step quickly to the ground. He drew his pistol but stayed in the saddle, thinking it might be more vital now to make a quick flight than to hide.

He expected a posse to come rushing at him through the brush. Instead he saw one horseman spurring toward him, still perhaps a hundred yards away. He tightened his grip on the pistol, not certain whether he could bring himself to use it.

Then he saw something else . . . a cow . . . no, a bull, also running in his direction.

He realized that the rider was not after Chacho, he was chasing that bull. The man's arm was swinging. At the distance Chacho could not see the rope, but he knew it must be there. The bull cut back into the brush, and the horseman followed him. Chacho heard a crashing of timber, an angry bellow, the scream of a horse. A man shouted. There was more threshing in the brush. Then the bull came out, running. Again, Chacho could not see the rope, but he could see the dust raised by the trailing end. The cowboy had caught him but the rope had broken.

Well, it was a thing that had happened to Chacho a few times; he could sympathize with the cowboy, but not a lot. Because of that rider, Chacho now would have to make a wide swing through this brush to make sure he was not seen. This close to Carrasco's, he did not like to waste the time.

He saw something in the edge of the thicket where the bull had come out. The cowboy was probably trying to rebuild a new loop in his considerably shorter rope, Chacho figured, and go after that bull again. *Bueno*, then he would be too busy to notice Chacho.

But only the horse came out. There was no man. The horse moved oddly, its head down. It stopped, swaying, fighting to stay on its feet. Like it had been shot, Chacho thought. But there had been no shot. He waited a long time to see what else might come out of that brush. Nothing did. Where was the man?

The longer Chacho waited, the more certain he was that a man was hurt in that brush, maybe even dead. Cautiously, knowing he shouldn't, he began moving toward the horse. He saw a gaping wound in the animal's side, the lifeblood draining. He saw the broken, frazzled rope hanging from the saddlehorn, its frayed end trailing on the bloody ground.

The horse went down. It would be a mercy for Chacho to put a bullet in its head, but he was afraid someone might hear the shot.

He looked at the brush, not wanting to go in there. He knew he ought to ride way around and continue on his way. Whatever had happened, it was none of his business. He had urgent business of his own. He started to ride on, but something held him. He thought for a moment he heard a sound. He turned his ear to listen, but there was nothing except the buzzing of the flies, already drawn to the horse's warm blood.

Chacho shouted in Spanish, "Who is in there? Where are you?"

He was not sure he heard any answer. The horse was groaning. Chacho shouted again. This time he was sure he heard something besides the dying horse. Pistol cocked, he pushed the black into a slow walk, working his way through the brush.

He found a small clearing, and in the midst of it a young boy half sat, half lay, holding his arms to his sides. He looked at Chacho, a terrible pain in his eyes, his face drained of color. On the ground where he lay was a grow-

ing pool of blood.

"My God!" Chacho whispered and swung quickly to the ground. The black horse snorted, rollers in its nose. It did not like the smell of blood. Chacho kept a firm grip on the reins lest it jerk loose and run away.

Kneeling, he decided this boy was about the age of Diego Bustamante's son Anselmo. But there was a difference. This boy was Anglo, not Mexican.

Chacho said, "Do you not know better, boy, than to

rope such a bull when you are by yourself? Such a bull can kill you."

The boy tried to move but groaned in pain. He tried to talk, but nothing came except a brief sobbing.

A damnfool stunt but just like a kid, Chacho thought, trying to tackle a job too big for him. Most grown men would hesitate to do what this fool boy had done. Chacho had done a few things like this in his own boyhood; it was a wonder he had lived to be grown.

This boy wouldn't live if he stayed here.

The boy finally managed to say, "Fetch me my horse."

"Your horse has been gored even worse than you are. Where is your home? How far?"

The boy turned a little, grimacing, and pointed. "Three . . . four miles."

Chacho's first thought was that he might find the boy's house and send help back. But he doubted he could give directions anyone could follow and find this place without a loss of much time. He saw no particular landmarks for reference. There was a brushy sameness about all of this stretch of country.

He was suddenly angry with himself. *Dammit, why didn't I go on by as I started to? What I didn't know could not have bothered me. I could ride on now and forget about it. He is just another gringo. If he dies it will save a good Mexican from having to kill him someday.*

He told himself he should get on the black and ride away, but it was a hopeless argument. He had seen.

He cursed himself for his stupidity, and then he cursed himself for his bad luck. If he had come a little earlier or a little later or had ridden just a little to the east or west he would not be facing this dilemma.

What if he saved this gringo boy's life and lost his own?

He cursed the boy for being so stupid.

His anger finally ran out, though anxiety took its place. He looked back over his shoulder as if he expected to see a dozen Rangers coming up behind him.

If he tarried long, he might.

157

"You are bleeding badly," he told the boy. "That horn must have gone in deep. If we do not stop that blood, or at least slow it, you have no chance." He tore off the boy's shirt, ripped a couple of large pieces out of it and wadded them, shoving them into the wound. *Like plugging the bunghole in the barrel,* he thought. A darker thought followed. The boy might be bleeding as much inside as outside. If so, probably not even a doctor could save him; certainly not a fugitive Mexican.

"Do you think you have strength enough to stand?" The boy said he would try. Chacho got his strong hands under the boy's arms. The boy made it to his feet, but he could not have stood if Chacho had not been holding him up.

"Now to get you into the saddle." That would be a fair chore in itself. The black horse still had the rollers in its nose. It kept shying away from the boy. Chacho shouted a Mexican oath at him and jerked on the reins, not enough to hurt the horse's mouth but enough to show him which one was going to be boss. The boy tried to raise his left foot for the stirrup, and Chacho had to help him. Firmly holding the reins, he gave the boy a boost that put him up into the saddle. The trembling hands managed to grab the saddlehorn. Chacho swung up behind him, taking a firm seat just over the black's hips. The black humped a little, threatening to pitch. It was not used to carrying double. Chacho promised in no uncertain terms to gut him and feed him to dogs if he made a single jump. He thought the horse's former owner must have taught him a good vocabulary, because the black calmed down.

"Where did you say your home is?" Chacho asked. The boy, hunching over the horn and holding his arms tight against his sides, managed to point vaguely with his chin. Chacho touched his heels to the black's flanks, almost causing the horse to spill them both.

His strongest impulse was to run, to try to make up for lost time. He kept looking back over his shoulder. He had never seen anyone back there, but he sensed that someone was. This long flight had roused instincts he never knew he had. He was convinced that someone was not only behind him but close behind him.

He had heard that gringo lawmen sometimes used dogs that had a powerful sense of smell and could track a man anywhere, even over rocks, over rivers. He had never seen such a dog, but he had never talked over a gringo telephone, either, yet he knew they existed. Could it be that the officers were using such dogs to trail after him? Or could it be that there was even a gringo who had the smelling talent for himself?

The thought made him shiver.

It also made him impatient. He moved the black into a trot, but he soon had to rein him back down to a walk. The boy was groaning. The trot jolted him painfully. This black did have a rough gait, not smooth and easy like the sorrel mare. Chacho touched the rough bandage he had made from the boy's shirt. He could feel the blood soaking through; his hand came away sticky.

Presently he found a well-worn cattle trail and reasoned that it should lead to the ranch headquarters. All cattle trails eventually converged on water. The boy said nothing. Chacho thought he had probably been unconscious a big part of the time. He slumped forward, mostly dead weight.

Chacho had hoped the boy would gain enough strength that he could be left somewhere near the house and walk in by himself. That was a vain hope, he knew now.

All the time he rode, opposing forces waged a quiet inner war. On the one side he told himself he was a fool; this boy had gotten into trouble through his own rashness, and Chacho owed him nothing. The Rangers were back there somewhere, closing the gap; he sensed that with a cold dread that settled in his stomach. On the other side he told himself that to have gone off and left this boy would have been the same as killing him. There was already more on Chacho's conscience than one man should have to bear. The knowledge that he had left a bull-gored boy to die would be a sorry thing to carry into his old age.

He came into sight of a set of ranch buildings and corrals.

For some time he had seen the two big Eclipse windmills and had known where the ranch would be. He drew up a couple of hundred yards from the house to look the place over. He saw horses in a corral and saddles lying on the ground. This was a cow outfit. He guessed the working hands were in for the noon meal. He hoped, at least, that this was the case. He hoped he had not ridden into a nest of *rinches*.

"Boy," he asked, "are those cowboys, or are they Rangers?"

The boy made no answer. He was in no condition to hear anything or to answer anything. Chacho put his hand on the bandage. Wet.

This could not go on much longer, not if the boy was to live.

But damn! *What if they are Rangers instead of cowboys?*

And even if they *were* cowboys, they would find the Rangers and tell them.

Chacho knew that from a personal standpoint it would be to his advantage to leave the youngster out here, per- haps near the corral, where the men would find him when they came to catch horses for the afternoon's work. That might be right away, or it might be an hour.

The boy groaned, stirring a little, trying to fight his way to consciousness. He was not dead yet, but in an hour he could be. Chacho knew what he had to do; he had known it ever since he had come upon the accident. All that argu- ing with himself had been for nothing; he had not been able to leave the boy then and he could not leave him now. There was nothing to be done except to ride up to that ranchhouse and pray a little.

As a precaution he drew the pistol and found the grip sticking to his hand. Blood.

"Hello! In the house!" he shouted. "Come out and get your boy!"

He heard no response. Probably they had not heard him. He took a firm grip on the reins in case the black should shy, and he fired the pistol into the air. "Come get your boy!"

The door swung open. A middle-aged gringo appeared with a rifle in his hand. Chacho's impulse was to shoot him. He would have, if that rifle had ever pointed his way. But the man's eyes went wide as he recognized the boy. His jaw dropped.

"Johnny!" he shouted. "What you doin' with my Johnny?"

"He is hurt," Chacho said.

The man flung the rifle away and came running. He moved so fast that he startled the black horse. Chacho almost lost his hold. The man reached up with both hands, afraid the boy would fall. Other men rushed out of the house. They gathered around Chacho and the black horse. Several of them gently brought the boy down from the saddle.

The gray-haired man knelt by his son, tearing away the bloody bandage. He swore and looked up, angry.

"What happened? Did you shoot him?" There was a sudden threat in his eyes. Chacho was glad he still held the pistol. There was a look to these gringos . . . at one word from that old man they would pull Chacho from his saddle and tear him to pieces.

"No," Chacho said. "He was gored by a bull. The bull also killed his horse."

Somebody said, "That's no bullet wound. A horn made that, sure as hell."

The anger left the old man. "Let's get him into the house. Somebody's got to ride for a doctor. We got to stop that bleedin' or we'll lose him." He looked up at Chacho. "I owe you for this, amigo. Come on in and get somethin' to eat. If you need a job. . . ."

Chacho shook his head. "No. I have to go on." He started backing the black away. He still held the pistol.

One of the cowboys said, "Walt, you know who that is? That's the Mexican they all been huntin' for."

Somebody ran to grab the rifle the rancher had brought out. Chacho fired the pistol and kicked up dirt in front of him.

The rancher shouted, "Leave him alone! All of you, leave him alone!"

One of the cowboys protested, "But he's the one they're after."

"He brought my boy home. I don't give a damn what he's done somewhere else." The cowboys accepted the rancher's order. They watched silently while Chacho backed the black a little farther.

The rancher looked Chacho in the eye. "Hombre, nobody here will bother you. I promise you that. Nobody here will tell that they saw you. I hope you make the river."

Chacho's mouth was too dry for him to give an answer. He looked at the old man and wondered if he could believe him. It would be hard for him to believe *any gringo*, ever again.

But he wanted to believe this one.

He managed to say, "I hope the boy lives." He turned the black and left in a lope. He had much time to make up for before he got to Carrasco's.

FIFTEEN

Kelly Sadler's first thought when they found the dead horse was that there had been a shoot-out. Chacho Fernandez' incredible luck had finally run its course. But that gaping slash in the horse's side had not been made by a bullet. Perhaps the horse had somehow run into a jagged and ungiving limb. More likely, judging from that broken rope, he had been gored by whatever had been on the other end, in the loop.

Kelly placed his palm on the horse's neck. "Still a little warm."

Joe Florey grunted, looking at the tracks. "That Chacho, he come right by here."

Kelly had ridden with the rifle in his lap through most of these long days, but never had he felt the probable need for it stronger than now. Somewhere ahead, and not very far, was the man they had spent all this time trying to find. The trail was warmer now than it had ever been.

"Better watch close from now on, Joe."

"You watch. That's your job."

They found the clearing and the torn-up ground, a muddle of horse and cow tracks, or possibly those of a bull. They found a pool of sun-dried blood that appeared to be separate from the one left by the staggering horse. Around it were boot tracks. And finally, heading more west than south, the tracks of the horse they had trailed from Hermoso.

Joe Florey puzzled awhile. Finally his eyes lifted to Kelly's. "You figure this the way I do?"

Kelly was incredulous, knowing what Joe was thinking. He could see for himself what the tracks indicated, but he could not accept it. "He wouldn't do it. Him, a killer with the whole country lookin' for him? He wouldn't."

"I reckon he did. Somebody was hurt here, and that Mexican *killer* picked him up."

Kelly could not reconcile the idea. "Another Mexican, probably."

"Probably." Joe pointed his chin. "They went yonder-way, and not too long ago. You watch, Kelly. You watch real good."

Presently, somewhere ahead, they heard a shot, and in a minute, another. It was difficult to judge the distance; it might have been a couple of miles, or even three or four.

Joe Florey glanced at Kelly. "The hell with the tracks. Let's ride!"

They put their horses into a lope. Shortly they began to see two windmills standing up high above the brush. They knew within reason that this would be where the shots were fired.

"Only two," Kelly mused. "Couldn't of been much of a fight."

"Might not've been no fight atall. Might've been a shade one-sided. Maybe when we get there we'll find our Mexican dead."

"Or somebody else," Kelly pointed out.

Perhaps Fernandez had killed somebody. The thought brought a feeling oddly akin to relief. The idea of Chacho

Fernandez pausing in his flight to help some stranger simply didn't fit the mental image Kelly had of him. It just was not an appropriate way for a man to act after having shot and killed a good man like Griffin Holliday. If Fernandez had killed somebody here, that was bad luck for whoever happened to be the victim, but at least the Mexican was comfortably back to form.

They came in sight of the ranch buildings. Seeing no activity around the barns or corrals, Kelly and Joe rode toward the main house. Quietly, automatically, they spread a little way apart as they approached. Kelly glanced at the ground. Near the door he saw a bloody piece of rag. He glanced at Joe; Joe had also seen it.

Kelly stepped down quickly and put the horse between himself and the door. He waited until Joe Florey had followed suit, then called, "Anybody in the house?" He aimed the rifle at the door.

The door opened slowly. A gray-haired man stood there. "You fellers put them rifles away. You got no need for them here."

"Where's he at?" Kelly demanded. "Where's Fernandez?"

"Who? Who's Fernandez?"

Kelly stared at the rancher, not sure what to make of the situation. It occurred to him that somebody might be inside the house, holding a rifle on the man. "Can you step out away from the door?"

The rancher said, "Sure," and did so without any apparent fear.

Kelly was more puzzled than ever, but he let the muzzle of his rifle point up away from the door. "There's somethin' wrong here."

Joe Florey said, "You're damn right there is. I see that horse's tracks, all over the yard."

"You sure, Joe? You sure it's the same tracks?"

"I may not read writin' as good as some people, but I read tracks. These are the ones we've followed ever since Hermoso."

An awful thought came to Kelly. Maybe they had followed the wrong horse all this time. Maybe Chacho Fernandez had never been within forty miles of this place.

But he dismissed the notion. They had been after Fernandez. They had been so close they could almost smell him. Sternly Kelly said, "We're after a man who killed a sheriff. You sayin' you've seen no such man?"

The rancher replied evenly, "We've seen no killer here."

Kelly studied him hard and had a strong feeling that much was being left unsaid. He could see the lie in the man's eyes. "I'm goin' in the house and look around, Joe. You watch out here and cover me."

"All right, Kelly."

The rancher protested. "That's my house. You've got no business in there."

The more he thought about it, the more Kelly knew he had better go in. "I'm a Texas Ranger, mister. Give me any trouble and you're in trouble. You better stay right where you're at."

"My boy's in there. He's been hurt. There's nobody here that you need that rifle for."

"I'll judge for myself."

Kelly pushed the door wider open with his foot and stood back, waiting to see if anything would happen. When nothing did, he went in, the rifle ready. He blinked, letting his eyes become accustomed to the poor light. What he saw brought him up short. A boy lay on a cot, his side freshly bandaged. He appeared to be unconscious. Two cowboys knelt over him, their sleeves up, their hands bloody. A pan of reddened water and a dozen spoiled cloths were on the floor.

Kelly saw no threat. He lowered the rifle. "What happened?"

One of the cowboys said, "Gored. We've sent for help."

"Who brought him in?" Kelly asked, knowing the answer before he asked the question. The cowboys said nothing. Behind Kelly the rancher said, "One of the boys found him."

Kelly turned, frowning. "Name of Chacho Fernandez?"

Nobody said anything. Nobody had to. The answer was as plain as if they had written it down. Kelly looked at the rancher, "I don't believe I heard your name."

"It's Johnson."

"Mister Johnson, whatever that man has done for you, it doesn't offset the fact that he shot and killed a damn good sheriff."

Johnson said stubbornly, "I don't know anything about anybody gettin' killed. All I know is that my son is alive, and he's got a good chance to *stay* alive. You'll find no one here to help you, Ranger."

Joe Florey stood in the doorway, listening. "I think we'd just as well go, Kelly."

Kelly nodded reluctantly. Probably the most they could tell him was what direction the Mexican went, and the tracks would tell that anyway. "Sorry about your boy, Mister Johnson. I hope he makes it."

"He'll make it. I ain't *lettin'* him go."

Joe pulled out of the door, and Kelly followed him through it. He shoved his foot into the stirrup and swung into the saddle. The rancher Johnson stood in the doorway. "Ranger, mind if I ask you somethin'?"

"What's that?"

"If that Mexican is the kind of killer you say he is, why would he go out of his way to help a hurt boy — a gringo boy at that — and risk his own life doin' it?"

"I couldn't answer that."

"I ain't askin' you to answer it. I'm just askin' you to *think* on it if you ever have occasion to look at him over the sights of your rifle. Think hard before you pull that trigger."

Kelly and Joe rode a long way in brooding silence. At length Joe said, "I been studyin' a right smart on what that rancher asked you about Fernandez."

"You come up with any answer?"

"No. I think back on that cowboy he could've killed a few days ago when he was needin' a horse so bad. He didn't do

167

it. Then I think on the boy in that ranch house. Easiest thing would've been to've rode off and left him where he found him. He didn't do it. The longer I think on it the bigger the question gets. Maybe you got an answer."

"I don't need one. I'm just doin' a job, is all."

"What you've seen hasn't changed you any?"

"He's wanted. That hasn't changed." Kelly's eyes narrowed. "Seems to me you've changed, though. You've been softenin' on him, Joe."

Joe Florey thought about that awhile. "Odd, how it happens sometimes. The longer you track a man the more you get to feelin' like you know about him. You follow in his footsteps long enough, you start to get a kinship to him. You see him dfferent, sometimes, than when you started." He paused, watching Kelly. "The first day out, you said you intended to kill him. You still figurin' on it?"

Kelly did not answer.

SIXTEEN

The black was tiring badly. Chacho hoped Carrasco had a good one he could use the rest of the way to the river. He doubted the smuggler would be generous enough to give him a horse. Carrasco would go along to see that Chacho made the other side of the river, and that would probably be the end of it. Once Chacho was safely across he would be on his own, broke and afoot. Up to now he had not devoted much time or worry to what he would do once he was in Mexico; he had figured that problem could be deferred until it became a fact. He had known from the beginning that the odds were extremely long against his getting there. Now he was so near Mexico he fancied he could smell the river, although it was still an hour's hard ride beyond Carrasco's. Now he began to feel that he *was* going to make it after all. Now the concern over what he would do on the other side was beginning to assume an importance of its own.

They had big ranches in Mexico, just as in Texas, and

169

surely they needed a man who had Chacho's skill with the horses. If not, they had cotton in Mexico. He was not too proud to hoe the fields and pick cotton. One way or another, he would survive.

He had fallen into a familiar trail an hour or so after leaving the Johnson place. It led him to a watering where he had several times stopped to rest a set of horses bound for new owners across the river. He paused there a short while to let the black rest. Chacho rolled a brown-paper cigarette and sat on his heels and thought of the future.

It would be lonely in Mexico, no family or old friends to help take the edge off the strangeness. Of late he had tried not to think of Luisa Aguilar any more, and instead he found himself thinking more and more of the Bustamante girl Juanita. He had never paid a great deal of attention to her before. She had paled in Luisa's light. He had never thought of her in terms of a woman, taking a woman's place with a man. He was not in love with her. The thing that had happened between them had been, on his part at least, a response to the hunger and need of the moment. But a man could fall in love with a woman like that if he let himself.

It was something to think about, when he was settled and secure, when he could afford himself the luxury of a woman. Perhaps he might decide to send for her. If — and the thought always brought a coldness to him — if she were still alive. He had never stopped wondering about the outcome of all that shooting at the Bustamante place. It was like those damned *rinches* to kill everybody they came across!

He pushed to his feet and cast away the brown stub of the cigarette. "A little more, black horse, then you can rest and fill your belly until you look like a mare in foal." He remounted, took a look behind him, and set out in a long trot toward the south.

There was little to let a stranger know he was approaching a house if he did not notice the convergence of the livestock trails. He would suddenly come out of a heavy thicket and there would be Carrasco's, a squatty rock house, a set of brush corrals, an open shed that served for a barn. Behind the shed was a stack of hay, which Carrasco managed somehow to replenish every year from a small field. How a man could coax a crop out of this rain-shy ground had always been a mystery to Chacho.

He was coming upon the place from the back side, by the corrals and the shed. He was curious to see what kind of horses Carrasco might have, for he intended to borrow one. If there was anything Carrasco liked better than warring against the gringos, it was having a good horse. Almost always there were from two to a dozen in his corrals.

It struck Chacho odd, then, to find the pens empty, the gates thrown open. It was not like Carrasco to be afoot.

What Chacho had done, probably, was to catch Carrasco gone from home. Even now he would bet the old reprobate was trying to skin somebody in a horse-trade. That was fine for Carrasco but a bitter disappointment for Chacho.

I need a fresh horse; I had counted on his being here.

He indulged in a few harsh thoughts about the old smuggler until he considered that Carrasco could have had no way to know he was coming. There had been no way to send him word.

I'll have to make it to the river by myself, and this black will have to carry me.

If he could not get a fresh horse from Carrasco, at least he ought to find some food in the house. Surely the old bandit would not begrudge him that, in view of the many horses Chacho had brought to him in times past.

Riding toward the house, he sensed that something was different. He could not quite put his finger on it for a moment. Then he knew . . . the dogs. That damned Carrasco always had several barking dogs to bedevil a man before he got within a hundred yards of the place. They were a protection against surprise.

Where were those dogs?

He was halfway between the shed and the house, out in the clearing, when he heard a horse nicker in the brush to his left. He felt relief. He could catch a horse for himself, let Carrasco figure out what had happened to it.

As he neared the heavy brush he could see a horse . . . no, he could see four horses. They were saddled and tied. And the saddles were not Mexican, they were the gringo type with high, thin horns and a cantle that looked like a moldboard plow.

Something was wrong here, he knew suddenly. Something was terribly wrong.

He heard something from the house and looked back. Four men were running toward him, guns in their hands. The *rinches!* The damned *rinches!* He drummed heels against the black's ribs and set him into a lope.

He heard a fusillade of shots and felt the black horse break stride, stumble, then catch himself.

A trap! They had him in a trap!

No, not yet they hadn't. If he could make it into those thickets to the south, he still had a chance. The men were running toward the tied horses they had hidden in the brush.

Chacho cursed himself now for not thinking faster. He could have broken those horses loose and left them afoot; now he had missed that chance. All he could do now was to try to outrun them.

Slugs whined into the brush.

Goddamn them, don't they ever quit? I've almost made the river! I've been through hell to get this far. I've earned it now. Why won't they quit and leave me alone?

The black began to falter. He was hit. Chacho saw the blood running. In a minute the horse would go down, and he would not get up.

Chacho glanced back. He could hear men shouting as they caught their horses and spurred after him, but he could not see them. Well, they could not see him, either. He swung his right leg over the horse's neck, kicked his left foot out of the stirrup and took a jump at a small switch-type mesquite. He landed on his feet but went down on his hands and knees. The thin green limbs were full of sap and gave way under the impact, although sharp thorns stung his flesh. He shouted at the black and waved his hat, sending the horse on in a run, what little run was still left in it. He saw a heavy clump of brush he thought should hide him and sprinted for it. He flopped on his stomach just as the first two riders came into sight.

He held his breath as they rode by him in a hard run, pistols in their hands. He watched them pass the spot where he had jumped. One of the limbs had broken as he landed, but they took no notice of it. Two more riders came spurring, trying desperately to catch up.

Four horses. That was all he had seen in the brush. Unless someone remained at the house afoot, this was all of them.

He crouched there, breathing hard, trying to force down the panic that threatened him. This was the closest call he had had. It wouldn't take them long to run down that black horse. When they found it without a rider, they would come back looking. This brush was not thick enough to hide him when they started combing.

He tried to remember Carrasco's place . . . tried to recall if there was any good hiding place around it.

Sundown would come soon. If he could hold out until full dark, they would never catch him. He could walk to the river from here. How he would cross it he did not know; he was no swimmer. But he could find a way, he had little doubt of that. Get him to that river and he would cross it if he had to walk on the water!

But where to hide that they would not find him before dark? He struck out running, making the edge of the brush and pausing there a moment before breaking into the open. He thought of the haystack; he could crawl under it and cover himself with hay. But he rejected the notion. If he thought of it that easily, so might they. He cringed at the thought of being stabbed by a probing pitchfork.

The house, then. He recalled that he had heard talk

173

about Carrasco having a hidden getaway tunnel that led under the house and out to the brush behind the shed. He had never seen it . . . there had been no occasion . . . but perhaps he could find it.

He heard men shouting in the brush. They had found the black horse, more than likely, and they would soon be combing the chaparral. He had no more time to lose. He sprinted for the house, knowing his tracks would show if they had the eyes to look for them. But he had no way to cover them nor time to do it. He could only hope these tracks would be overlooked amid all the others that had been made here.

He hit the open door in a dead run. He started to close it after him but realized they might remember it had been open when they left it. He stopped with his back against the rock wall, breathing hard while his eyes adjusted themselves to the dim light. Where was the hidden door to that tunnel?

Chacho's heart sank. He saw an open hole toward a corner, its square wood cover standing tilted against the wall, a piece of goathide carelessly thrown back beside it.

Those damned *rinches*, they had found Carrasco's tunnel. Or perhaps they had forced Carrasco to show it to them.

Chacho could not hide in the hole now. But perhaps at least he could use it to get out to the shed and beyond, and find someplace he could hide. He walked over to the hole and started to climb down the narrow ladder.

He stopped, and he gagged. At the bottom he saw Carrasco, or what was left of him, crumpled in the grotesque manner of a Mexican marionette carelessly allowed to fall. With him lay his dogs in a bloody heap.

Chacho could not go down in that hole now. He could not bring himself to wriggle past that dead man and those dogs.

He went back to the door, fighting down a heavy wave of nausea. He leaned out cautiously to look for sign that anyone was coming back. He saw no one, but he realized how far he had to run in the open to reach the shed and the corrals. They would have to be far away or blind to miss seeing him.

He studied the brush arbor that butted up against the side of the rock bouse. He considered for a moment getting on top of the arbor and lying flat, but he knew that from any distance he could probably be seen; the arbor was not high enough off the ground.

The house! If he could not hide under it, why could he not hide on top of it? It was of the flat-roofed type common to the Mexican people in this section of the country. It had just enough slope to let the infrequent rains run off through drains strategically placed on the back. The sides of the house stood a foot or more above the flat roof. If he lay on his stomach he could not be seen by anyone on the ground, or even anyone on horseback.

He took one more cautious look around, then moved out the door, hugging the wall. He grabbed onto the corner post of the arbor and swung himself up. The post had been in the ground a long time. It cracked and gave a little under his weight. He landed first on top of the arbor, then climbed over the adjoining wall and onto the dirt-covered roof. One of the wall stones jarred loose. He tried to catch it, but he was too late. It fell, knocking a small hole through the dead brush that made up the top of the arbor, then thudded to the ground, taking bits of dead branches with it.

Chacho swore under his breath but knew there was nothing he could do about it now. All he could hope for was that they kept looking for him out there until dark. Perhaps they would never guess that he might circle back and hide at the house.

If God stayed with him, as He had done so far, Chacho would yet make the river.

SEVENTEEN

Joe Florey was bent in the saddle, watching the horse tracks, when the shots exploded a little way ahead. Instinctively he swung to the ground, putting his horse between himself and the sound.

Kelly Sadler whipped his rifle to his shoulder. But he realized the shots had not been fired at them.

"He's run into somebody, Joe."

Florey had figured that out. "How far do you make it?"

"A few hundred yards."

The shots stopped as abruptly as they had started. Kelly's first reaction was of sorrow. "They got him, I suppose." He was surprised at himself. He wondered why he responded with sorrow rather than with relief that the long chase was over. He decided it was because of a feeling of waste. He had left his wife bereaved in Domingo ten days ago and had not had a chance to talk to her since, or find out how she was, to know whether the baby had come and how Tommie had managed without his being there. He and Joe

Florey had ridden themselves to the point of exhaustion for ten days, only to have someone else finish the chase ahead of them.

"A waste," he said, slump-shouldered. "We done the whole thing for nothin'."

Joe Florey had his left ear turned toward the source of the shots. "Maybe not. I hear horses runnin'. They wouldn't be runnin' if there wasn't somethin' to run after."

Florey remounted and gave his horse the spurs. For a minute Kelly didn't think he would catch up with him. He got a fleeting glimpse of a rock house in a clearing, but the noise was all ahead of them, somewhere out in that brush. He could hear men calling to each other. He heard no more shooting.

He thought under the circumstances it would not do to ride in on a run, unannounced. Somebody's trigger finger might be faster than his brain.

"Hello in yonder, whoever you are! We're comin' in. I'm a Ranger."

Someone shouted, "It's the Rangers comin'. Over this way, Rangers."

Kelly broke out of a thick clump of brush and found a man sitting on a horse, pistol in his hand but pointed into the air. Kelly blinked in surprise. This was one of the Domingo possemen he had last seen with Odom Willcox.

"What're you doin' here?" Kelly demanded.

"We had us that Mexican. Had him in our sights, but he got away. He's out here in this brush someplace. We'll get him, you can bet on that!"

Odom Willcox rode into the little clearing. He stared in surprise at Kelly and Joe. "How'd you-all get here?"

"We followed the tracks." Kelly said, wondering what kind of damnfool luck had placed Willcox and his bunch here at precisely the place where Chacho Fernandez would go.

"Well," Willcox said belligerently, "you can follow your own tracks back to where you come from. We've got him now. He's ours. We don't need you."

"You got him?" Joe Florey asked caustically. "Well, then, where's he at? Trot him out here so we can get a look at him."

"We got him trapped in the brush. Any minute now we'll flush him."

Kelly frowned. "It's awful heavy brush."

"He's afoot. We shot his horse. It's layin' right yonder."

Kelly rode to where Willcox pointed. He found a black horse lying on its side, its forefeet still moving a little, its eyes glazing.

Kelly said, "We'll join you in the hunt. He can't be far."

Willcox exploded. "No, Sadler, we don't need you. We don't want you. He's our Mexican now, and *we're* goin' to get him, not you. It's *me* that's goin' to ride into Domingo with that killer tied across a horse. I've worked for this. I've earned it. I ain't lettin' you take nothin' away from it."

Joe Florey was on the ground, looking around the dying horse. "He's right, Kelly. Let's let him alone."

Kelly turned angrily to the old man, not quite understanding him. "Joe, we won't leave here now!"

Florey remounted. "The man's right. He's earned it. I say let's leave him alone." He reined his horse around and said, "All right, Odom, we'll see you back in Domingo."

Kelly didn't know which man he felt most anger against, Willcox for trying to freeze him out or Joe for letting him do it. He shouted, "Joe, you come back here!"

But Joe Florey kept riding away. With an angry glance at Odom Willcox, Kelly loped off after Joe. Catching up to the old man, he loosed a heated barrage at him.

"Damn you, Joe, you're the one that's talked about how we oughtn't to kill that Mexican, how we ought to take him in for trial. You know they won't. They'll kill him on sight."

Florey looked Kelly straight in the eye. "They got to find him first. And they ain't goin' to. We are."

Kelly's mouth dropped open.

Florey said, "You ain't no tracker, Kelly. You won't be one if you live to be a hundred and six. Neither will them

179

other birds. That Mexican wasn't on that black horse when it went down. He jumped off sometime before that. We're goin' to find where he jumped off, and where he went, and we're goin' to catch ourselves one poor damn Mexican."

Joe wasn't three minutes in finding the place. He simply back-tracked the horse and kept watching for a sign while Kelly went back to his original protective function. Kelly felt shame for speaking so sharply. He should have known Joe Florey knew what he was doing. Joe Florey always knew what he was doing.

That, Kelly reflected, was how he got to be an old man. A lot of his companions of earlier years hadn't made it.

Joe reined up. Kelly saw what he was looking at, a broken mesquite limb. Kelly never would have noticed it on his own. Joe rode around it, bending in the saddle, then angled to a large clump of brush a few paces away. He pointed. "He laid here while they went by him. Then he picked up and ran. This way."

Kelly's heartbeat quickened. Anywhere out there, that Mexican could be lying in the brush, aiming at them. "Joe, you better watch out."

"I'll tell you again, you watch out," Joe said curtly. "That's your job."

They came to the edge of the clearing. There was no question that the boot tracks led toward the rock house. It might be worth a man's life to ride out into that opening now. But Joe Florey didn't hesitate. He kept riding, watching the ground, though Kelly suspected Joe had one eye on that house. The old man had his hand on his gunbutt.

180

Kelly was taking short breaths and running his tongue over lips dry as old leather. He had no choice but to follow Joe Florey, even if that meant moving into the muzzle of a gun. He couldn't let the old man ride in there alone.

They reined up in front. Kelly could feel the hair standing at the back of his neck. "You think he's inside?"

Joe Florey looked at the tracks in front of the door. "He went in, and he came back out." The old man's gaze went then to the brush arbor, and to the rock which lay under it amid a little pile of broken limbs and rotted timber. Slowly he dismounted, keeping the horse in front of him. He gave a little nod with his chin which Kelly took as a signal for him to move around to the other side of the house.

When Kelly had reached a position he heard Joe say without particularly raising his voice. "He's on top of the house, Kelly." Joe Florey shifted over then to a rough sort of gringo Spanish. "Come on down, Fernandez!"

Chacho Fernandez lay flat on the roof, fighting an almost overpowering impulse to raise up and look over the edge. He could hear the aging gringo voice in front of the house, and then he heard a different voice at the back, telling him to throw away whatever weapon he had and raise his hands. He lay still, or tried to, but all of a sudden his shoulders were shaking, and he found himself crying. All the pent-up tension of the last ten days broke loose. He clenched one fist and drummed it against the dirt roof.

For nothing! All of it had been for nothing!

They had him now. He was certain that when he raised up they would riddle him with bullets. That was the *rinche* way, was it not?

He cocked back the hammer of the pistol. His first intention was to jump up firing. They would kill him; he had no doubt of that. But if he went to hell, at least he might take one or two with him.

But he found no strength for it, no stomach. Too many had died already . . . his brother Felix, the sheriff, God knew how many Bustamantes, and Julio Carrasco . . . all for no good reason, all for a blackguard's lie.

If he killed one of these *rinches*, he would still die, and perhaps the other *rinches* would take out their anger on innocent Mexican people who had no part in this.

No, he would kill no one. Let them kill him, if they must, and let his own death be the end of it. He eased the hammer down and pitched the pistol out over the wall. He raised up a little, closing his eyes and making the sign of the cross. Slowly he pushed to his feet, steeling himself for the bullets.

He stood rigid, his eyes closed. He held his breath until his lungs seemed ready to explode. Nothing happened. Slowly he exhaled and opened his eyes. He looked down upon an old gray-haired man who barely showed behind the protection of a standing horse. The old man had a pistol pointed at Chacho. Chacho turned. Behind him, at the back of the house, was a younger man whose face was vaguely familiar. In a moment Chacho remembered. He had seen this man in the stagecoach, and later on the porch of Griffin Holliday. This *rinche* was the sheriff's friend.

Chacho blinked, not understanding. What of the rest of them? There had been four.

The Ranger at the back said in Spanish, "Climb down quickly before they see you."

Chacho was puzzled. Why should it matter now who saw him? But it was not in him to argue. It took a moment to get control over his fear-weakened legs and climb over the brush arbor. He dropped to the ground, going to his knees at the impact and staying there a little. His whole body was shaking.

"If you are going to kill me," he said, his voice quavering, "do it now. Do not make me die a minute at a time."

The two gringos looked at each other, then back at Chacho. The younger one said, "We are not going to kill you, although those others might."

"You are Rangers, are you not?" Chacho asked. "Rangers always kill a Mexican when they can."

Kelly Sadler shook his head, glancing at Joe Florey. "Where do they get that kind of a notion?"

Florey shrugged. "I guess there's always been a few Rangers who liked killin' a man, just as there's always been a few Mexicans who liked to cut a throat." He stared at Chacho Fernandez, an odd light in his eyes, almost an admiration. "He led us a hell of a chase, Kelly. Ten whole days of it. The longest trail I ever followed. He come within a little of gettin' clean away."

"We'd've caught him."

"You think so? I don't. If it hadn't been for Willcox, I

think he'd've made the river ahead of us. I still can't figure how Willcox got so lucky."

Kelly studied Fernandez and shook his head. "Doesn't look like so much now, does he? Doesn't look like a man who could get half the state of Texas into arms."

"No, he don't. Take a good look at him, Kelly, a hard look."

"What am I supposed to see?"

"If everything they've said is true, you're suppose to see a black-hearted killer. I don't. Do you?"

"What is a killer supposed to look like?"

"Not like this. Look at them eyes. You see a killer's eyes? No, you just see a poor unlucky Mexican who got himself pushed into a jam."

"He didn't have to kill Griff."

"Didn't he? The way things fell in on him, what choice did he have?" Joe didn't wait for an answer. "If he was a killer, why didn't he shoot that cowboy and take his horse? Why did he go out of his way to help that Johnson kid when he knew there was people on his trail?"

Kelly had no answer. It was not his place to have an answer; that was for the courts.

Joe said, "If he wasn't a Mexican, damn near any judge in the country would turn him loose."

"Bein' a Mexican ought not to have anything to do with it."

"It will, though. Look, Kelly, it ain't far to the river. I say we ought to let him go. Hell, I'll say more than that; I say we ought to help him get there."

"Turn a prisoner loose? We're officers of the law."

183

"You're an officer; I'm not. I just swore into a posse, is all. I hereby resign. All you got to do is go in that house and fix you a pot of coffee and sit down and wait. I'll see him to the river. You don't have to do a thing."

Kelly stared at Joe Florey. He knew he ought not to be surprised. He had seen this coming on; he had seen a gradual change in Joe's attitude along the trail, anger and recrimination turning slowly to a grudging acknowledgment of the man's spunk, and finally to an almost open admiration.

"Joe, there's no use arguin'. There is no argument."

"What would I have to do to get you to see it my way?"

Kelly thought a moment. "You'd have to shoot me."

Joe swore under his breath. "Goddamn you, you know I won't do that. I ought to, but I won't."

"Then we're losin' time talkin' about it. We've got to take him in."

"He'll never come to trial in Domingo. They'll hang him sure as hell."

Kelly pondered. "It doesn't have to be Domingo. We can take him to San Antonio instead. Nobody'll break him out of *that* jail."

Joe Florey gave up hard, but in the end he knew he had to. "All right, San Antonio." His eyes began to brighten. "Maybe we could get him a change of venue. If we could get the trial moved to San Antonio he'd stand a good chance."

"Maybe so," Kelly replied, "if you'd be willin' to work as hard to help him as you were to catch him."

"I will. How about you, Kelly? Will you help him?"

Kelly frowned, looking at the Mexican. "I'll have to be honest with you; I thought the world of Griffin Holliday, and my wife is his daughter."

Joe had to accept that. "But you won't work against him?"

"No, not against him."

"Then I believe we can work it. Get us to San Antonio and we can work it."

Joe looked off toward the brush. Occasionally someone shouted, way out in that chaparral. They seemed to be getting farther away. Joe said, "Odom Willcox ain't the smartest feller that ever come along, but he's not stupid. Sooner or later he'll figure out that we got his man, and he'll come on the run. We better get movin'." He handed Kelly his pistol and his rifle for safety, then motioned for Chaco Fernandez to swing up behind his saddle.

Kelly said, "Even with you ridin' double, I'd say we ought to make that Johnson ranch in a couple of hours. We'll get Johnson to lend us fresh horses. Then we'll strike out for the railroad. Somewhere up yonder we ought to find a train bound for San Antonio."

EIGHTEEN

There was no station at the Catclaw siding, just a set of railroad shipping pens used by the ranchers for miles around. The three riders had come upon the tracks an hour or so before sunup and had followed them north. The sun was halfway toward noon when they began to see the smoke of the engine, and then the rise of dust from the cattle pens. As they neared they could see a string of cattle cars on the siding. An engine was moving them into position one at a time for a crew of cowboys to load the cattle. That engine was pointed north.

Everybody in the pens stopped work to look at Kelly and Joe and Chacho Fernandez. Stopping at the fence, Kelly looked for a trainman. He picked him from the half dozen cowboys because of his cap and gray overalls. Kelly dismounted, steadying himself a minute before he tried to climb the fence. He was light-headed from loss of sleep. He knew his dusty clothes and stubbled face made him look like somebody who had crawled out from the rods beneath the cars. He climbed down inside the pen. He worked his way through the big three- and four-year-old Longhorn steers and walked up to the trainman.

"I'm Kelly Sadler, Texas Ranger. Where's this train goin'?"

The trainman looked him over with considerable curiosity. The cowboys were looking with equal curiosity at Chacho Femandez. Kelly knew what they were thinking,

The trainman said, "Well, it ain't goin' anywhere till we get all these cattle loaded. Then it's bound for Kansas grass."

It was just as well Joe Florey hadn't heard that, Kelly thought. Old Joe had long bemoaned the fact that the great trail drives had become a thing of the past. Nowadays a South Texas rancher could load his steers on a train and have them unloaded on the Flint Hills grass in a matter of days to put on summer tallow before heading for the Kansas City and Chicago packing houses in the fall. Damn trains had put many a good cowboy out of work.

Kelly said, "We have a prisoner we need to take to San Antonio. We could ride in your caboose."

The men still stared at Chacho Fernandez. A middle-aged man whom Kelly took to be the boss asked, "Is that the Mexican killer everybody's been lookin'for?"

Kelly didn't lie, exactly. He simply said, "Does he look like a killer?"

The ranchman thought about it. "No, I can't say as he does. I suppose he's a horsethief or somethin'?"

"He's been accused of that, but I doubt they'll make a case of it."

188

The trainman said he was sure the railroad wouldn't mind cooperating with the Rangers, and they would be glad to make room in the caboose. "It'll take a while, though," he warned. "We've still got a lot of cars to load, and ol' Ennis there, he's short-handed. Big part of his crew went off to help hunt for that Mexican everybody's after."

Weary, Kelly returned to Joe Florey and Chacho Fernandez and explained that they would ride the train when the cattle were all loaded. He would ask the cattle-men to take care of the horses and hold them for the ranch-er Johnson.

Chacho Fernandez stared at the cars. He said sadly, "I never rode a train. I always wanted to."

Joe Florey grunted. "Damn poor way to start."

As a precaution Kelly handcuffed Chacho to a fencepost. Then he flopped down with his back against a fence and tried to rest a little. He stared at Joe Florey. Now that Joe's manhunt was over, the old man's weariness showed in every line of his face, in his gray eyes, in the slump of his thin shoulders. This long ride had worn Joe Florey to a nub.

But Kelly would have to admit, if anyone pressed him, that he felt about as tired as Joe looked. Before long he found himself nodding off to sleep, and he shook his head, trying to clear his eyes. He pushed to his feet and walked around to try to work off some of the stiffness. He looked down the track, and his breath stopped for a moment.

Maybe it was nothing, but on the other hand maybe it was four horsemen coming along, far down the track. One time when he looked he could see them plainly. Next time he saw nothing. If he weren't so damn tired. . . .

He climbed up the second rail of the fence and saw that there were still three cars to be loaded. The work was going very slowly.

"Fernandez!" he said sharply. The Mexican looked up; he had never been asleep. Kelly said, "I understand you are a cowboy. If I took those cuffs off, would you help load these cattle on this train?"

The Mexican said he would, but Kelly could see the question in his eyes. Kelly said, "Look down the track. Do you see anything."

Fernandez squinted. "It could be horses."

Kelly hastened to unlock the cuffs. "If it's horses, it's probably Odom Willcox. If it's Willcox, he'll kill you right here in spite of all we can do. Let's help get this train loaded."

The cowman Ennis welcomed the help of the Mexican vaquero and the two Rangers. Kelly wondered what he would have thought of those helpers if he had known one of them actually was the notorious Chacho Fernandez. Three extra hands made the work go much faster.

The engine spotted the last car beside the loading chute. The cowboys slid the ramp into place and swung out the gates. Kelly climbed the fence for another look south.

There was no longer any question about it. He saw four horsemen, less than a quarter mile away.

He jumped down from the fence and whooped at the steers. He almost ran a couple of them over the slow-footed trainman. The last of the steers were on the car in a few minutes, and the big doors were slammed, locked and sealed.

Kelly knew it was his imagination, but he could almost recognize Odom Willcox from among the four horsemen now.

Anxiously he said to the trainman, "All ready to go."

The trainman glared, remembering the way he had had to climb up that chute in a hurry. "I'm in charge here. I'll say when we go."

Kelly's eyes narrowed. His voice went raspy with threat. "Then you had better say so pretty damn quick."

Kelly and Joe pitched their saddles onto the caboose. The one Chacho had used would go back to Johnson's. The conductor gave the signal, the engine whistled, and the train began to move. It crept at first. A dry-land terrapin could have outwalked it. Kelly stood on the rear platform and watched the four horsemen spurring, catching up.

The trainman saw them for the first time. "Friends of yours?"

Kelly said, "They're no friends of mine."

He carried his rifle cradled in his arm. He wouldn't use it, but he might sure as hell make somebody think he would.

The train slowly gathered speed. Still, for a while, the horsemen were gaining ground. Kelly could see Odom

Willcox frantically waving his hat. He couldn't hear for the noise of the train, but he would bet the boots on his feet that Odom was turning the air blue.

Gradually the train began moving faster. For a time the horsemen, spurring hard, seemed to be holding their own. Finally, inevitably, they began dropping behind. Kelly watched them until they were no more than specks far back in the distance. At last he wiped the sweaty palms of his hands on his dirty shirt and walked back into the swaying, bumping caboose.

Chacho Fernandez was handcuffed to a cot. He sat there with head down and shoulders slumped, thinking ahead, thinking back . . . who could ever tell what a Mexican was thinking? Joe Florey lay wearily on another cot, watching him with compassion.

Kelly pulled out a straight-backed wooden chair and sat down. He watched the Mexican in silence, then asked, "Do you have any idea how long a chase you led us?"

Chacho shook his head, not answering.

"Well, with all the zigzaggin' you done, and the back-trackin' and all, I'd say you made a good three hundred miles. It's hard to believe you did all that by yourself."

Chacho said "I was not by myself."

"What do you mean?"

The Mexican's eyes were incredibly sad. "Your friend the sheriff . . . he was with me all of the way."

Joe Florey turned his face toward the wall. Kelly thought if Fernandez could win the sympathy of an old manhunter like Joe, he would probably make other friends as he went along, people who would say he had been through hell enough. He had an ordeal ahead of him, but at the end of it perhaps he would come out all right.

Kelly waited a while before he spoke to Joe Florey. "Joe, I was wrong about you."

Joe turned around. "Wrong in what way?"

"I don't know if it'll help any at this late date, but I'll tell the board that I misjudged when I said you ought to be retired off of the force."

Joe's eyes were unreadable. "You admit it now, do you?"

Kelly nodded. "I was wrong. I'll do all I can to get your badge back."

Joe Florey studied on it, and a thin smile came across his tired, stubbled face. "Forget it. It's enough just hearin' you say it. Truth is, the best thing that ever happened to me was when they made me quit. I'm a way too old for this kind of foolishness."

AFTERWORD

On June 12, 1901, Gregorio Cortez, accused of horse theft, shot and killed W. T. "Brack" Morris, the sheriff of Karnes County, Texas, who had come to arrest him. Although Cortez shot the sheriff, he did not shoot the deputy, who was unarmed and who returned to town to set off a now-legendary manhunt that lasted for ten days.

During those ten days, Cortez was pursued by posses that at times included up to 300 men. He traveled 400 miles on horseback and more than 100 miles on foot, narrowly escaping capture time and again. Eventually, Cortez was captured near the Mexican border, but along the way he had become a folk hero to many, hidden and helped by people from all walks of life, and celebrated in stories and songs like "Corrido de Gregorio Cortez." He was a symbol of the struggle between the Anglos and Mexicans in South Texas. It is Cortez' story, considerably altered, that Elmer

Kelton has chosen to tell in *Manhunters*, though as he is careful to point out in his "Author's Note" his tale is "fiction and does not claim to follow the history of Cortez except in the broadest terms."

Manhunters was originally published in paperback by Ballantine Books in 1974 and is what those in the trade refer to as a "traditional western," although at the time of its release *The Day the Cowboys Quit* (1971) and *The Time It Never Rained* (1973), both distinctively non-traditional, had already appeared. These latter books marked Kelton's emergence from the genre ghetto; but Kelton, who began his fiction career writing for pulp magazines like *Ranch Romances*, has continued to write traditional westerns like *Manhunters* down to the present. It is instructive to see how he worked with the original source material in order to produce a quite satisfactory paperback.

In the first place, Kelton chose to make Chacho Fernandez, his stand-in for Cortez, an almost entirely sympathetic character. While in both stories it is the sheriff who fires the first shot, Cortez reportedly shot Brack Morris four times, then ran to the body and fired a fifth bullet into it. In *Manhunters*, Fernandez, who is unarmed, kills the sheriff entirely by accident in a struggle for the sheriff's pistol. And in the novel, Fernandez kills no one else, though it must have been hard for Kelton to resist the inherent drama of the real shoot-out which could have come straight out of a dime novel. Surrounded by a posse, Cortez, bootless and footsore, walked straight toward the mounted Gonzalez County Sheriff Robert M. Glover, firing his pistol until the lawman fell from the saddle. It was this second killing for which Cortez was convicted and for which he was sentenced to prison; he was acquitted of the murder of Morris, and by eliminating this second killing from the story, Kelton is able to provide an ending that hints that Fernandez may escape prison entirely.

In fact, Fernandez exhibits great compassion throughout the novel, feeling guilt not only for killing Morris but for the suffering he inadvertently causes those with whom he comes in contact, thanks to the ruthless tactics of some of the lawmen pursuing him. In spite of the actions of the law, however, Fernandez himself passes up the chance to kill a young cowboy in order to obtain his horse, and at one point he risks capture to return an injured Anglo boy to his ranch house so that he can receive medical attention. Nowhere does Fernandez intentionally harm anyone.

Kelton also emphasizes Fernandez' great love of horses, a characteristic Fernandez seems to have shared with his real-life counterpart. Fernandez' care and concern for the stout-hearted mare he had intended as a gift for the doe-eyed Luisa Aguilar are brought out again and again.

And what better way to gain sympathy for an outlaw protagonist than to put him in contention with a truly malevolent representative of law and order? Deputy Odom Willcox sees his mission as not so much to capture Fernandez as to kill him — and to kill anyone else who gets in the way. Even when Willcox's vicious stupidity results in the death of one of his own men in a crossfire, Willcox remains adamant in his desire to exterminate Fernandez: "He's bloodthirsty, Odom is," Joe Florey reports.

Joe Florey, on the other hand, represents the good side of the Anglo population. The old tracker, who has been forcibly retired from the Texas Rangers, is the first to realize that Fernandez is probably not quite such a cold-hearted killer as Willcox wants everyone to believe. As Florey patiently follows Fernandez' trail, he begins to admire his quarry and to see that Fernandez is both a clever and admirable adversary. He has some difficulty in convincing his companion, Ranger Kelly Sadler, of Fernandez' likely innocence, but eventually even Sadler begins to feel that Fernandez is not quite as guilty as he seemed at the beginning of the chase.

Along with the pursuit of Fernandez, the growing understanding between Florey and Sadler, and the developing respect they have for Fernandez, there are any number of subplots, including such components as Fernandez' love of Luisa (and the love of Juanita Bustamente for Fernandez), the birth of Sadler's first child, Willcox's overweening ambition to become sheriff, and Florey's resentment at having been forced out of the Rangers. Although some of these plots are never fully developed, each adds to the interest and texture of the story and fits seamlessly into the thrust of the pursuit.

Of course, Kelton was not interested in simply re-telling the story of Gregorio Cortez. That had been done already. Kelton presents a thoughtful look at the clash of Anglo and Mexican cultures in South Texas in the early part of the twentieth century, depicting attitudes that might not be too far off the mark even now. An often repeated thought on both sides before and during the manhunt might be phrased like this: "Who can ever know what an Anglo/a Mexican is thinking?" Misunderstandings and mistrust begin Fernandez' troubles, and misunderstandings and mistrust compound them, resulting not only in the shooting deaths of Fernandez' brother and the sheriff but in the other deaths that follow. Kelton makes it clear that all the blame is not on one side or the other. When it comes to intolerance, there is ample blame to go around.

Add to this culture clash the fact that modern inventions were beginning to affect the life of the ranchers, and the novel takes on still another layer of meaning. Fernandez' original plan, to turn north instead of south as everyone expects, is a sound one, and it might even have worked had it not been for the telephones found not only in towns but in some of the more prosperous ranch houses. Fernandez knows about telephones, but he has never used one. And he has never been entirely certain that they actually work, not until he sees a posse looking for him where no posses should have been.

Manhunters, then, is an action western with serious thematic underpinnings, a book rich in character and incident that at the same time deals with important questions of guilt and innocence, right and wrong, bigotry and tolerance. It both diverts and informs, providing in the process the best kind of popular entertainment.

Bill Crider
Alvin Community College

ABOUT THE AUTHOR

For more than fifty years, Elmer Kelton, who died on August 22, 2009, was Texas' most respected writer about the American West. Author of more than fifty novels, Kelton wrote both serious historical novels and what he called "powder burners." But whether writing serious fiction or genre fiction, Elmer Kelton's work was marked by careful craftsmanship and serious purpose. He was recognized by his peers as "the Best Western Writer of All Time." He was awarded seven Spur Awards by the Western Writers of America, the Levi Strauss Golden Saddleman Award from WWA, four Wrangler Awards from the National Cowboy & Western Heritage Museum, and the Lon Tinkle Award from the Texas Institute of Letters for Lifetime Achievement. For many years, he combined his work as a novelist with a distinguished career as an agricultural journalist, spending more than twenty years as a columnist and editor with *The Livestock Weekly*. His passing leaves a large gap in Texas letters.